UNEASY

RIDER

UNEASY RIDER

by

John Scherber

The Fourteenth Book in the Murder in México Series

San Miguel Allende Books
San Miguel de Allende, GTO, México

ACKNOWLEDGMENTS

Any book starts as an idea, and by its completion becomes a joint effort.

Thanks to all the following:
Al Rabi Arredondo Nova for the cover photo.
Lander Rodriguez for the cover design.
Julio Mendez for website design.

For equestrian tips and corrections: Howard Haynes, Rafael Lavista, Michael Martin, Amy Spencer, Cristina Valencia, Nicole Zijlstra.

To my writer's work group for constant input and critiques: Florence Grende, Christina Johnson, Michael Landfair, Marcia Loy, Dr. Cynthia Miller, and Lynda Schor.

For Texas cultural input, Colleen Sorenson.
For editing and equestrian input, my wife, Kristine Scherber.

ISBN 978-0-9906551-1-4

San Miguel Allende Books
San Miguel de Allende, GTO, México.

www.sanmiguelallendebooks.com

Also by John Scherber

FICTION

The Devil's Workshop
Eden Lost
The Amarna Heresy
Beyond Terrorism: Survival

NONFICTION

San Miguel de Allende: A Place in the Heart
A Writer's Notebook: Everything I Wish Someone
Had Told Me When I Was Starting Out
Into the Heart of Mexico: Expatriates Find Themselves off the
Beaten Path
Living in San Miguel: The Heart of the Matter

AUTHOR'S NOTE

I want to thank all the members of the San Miguel equestrian community who helped me correct the detail of this book. The remaining errors are all mine.

While some may be tempted to see themselves in this story, the truth is that no real person was used in a speaking role as a character here, even if a few might seem to be partially visible on the sidelines in passing. The San Miguel horse world I have depicted in these pages is populated more by imagined characters, a mix of pygmies and giants, saints and villains, with a few normal people included for accent and contrast. In that respect they resemble all of us and none of us. As purely fictional beings they are freer to act out their fantasies, as I am in recruiting them for this drama.

The modern horse, through many generations of selective breeding, has become an extension of the human ego, an astounding feat of genetic engineering.

-Derek Hamilton,
Wonders of Modern Science

For Kristine

CHAPTER ONE

The dark-skinned boy whose body lay crumpled at my feet that morning was clearly dead. He had arced through the air to land about thirty meters from the nearest derailed boxcar. On impact, his head had been driven in between his shoulders. When his backpack straps ripped free, the bag burst open ten or twelve feet past the body.

As word began to circulate about the train wreck behind Rancho Aria, many people assumed it was the daily banana train up from Cocobamba, in the state of Tabasco. That wasn't true, because the banana train runs on the tracks across the valley, on the other side of the Rio Laja. This derailment had occurred with the Devil Train on its sad biweekly run north from Guatemala. Local people call it the Devil Train because of the poor devils who cling to the tops of the boxcars. I arrived on the scene about two hours after the accident happened.

My partner, Maya Sanchez, both in life and in the Paul Zacher Agency that bears my name, called me upon her arrival at the rancho to ride just before nine o'clock. Our other partner, Cody Williams, would catch up with us later, since he was still talking to the rescue crew closer to the wreck. After thirty years as a police detective in Illinois, procedural matters always caught his attention. His car was parked near the fatal crossing. We had driven out together right after Maya's call.

A minor track repair fifty kilometers to the south delayed the Devil Train on this morning's trip for three and a half hours. It normally passes San Miguel de Allende, our town in the state of Guanajuato, México, just before four in the morning, and I hear it if I'm lying awake thinking about a case. That's why, at 7:07 A.M. on a Tuesday, when the Devil Train was crossing a feeder road that came down out of the *cantera* quarries northeast of town, it was still more than three hours late and going much too fast. This information only came out later.

La Estrella was the name of the battered yellow dump truck that hit the train. Its forty-year-old heavy-duty chassis carried an eighteen-year-old box that was overloaded on every run with several tons too much rough-cut stone. The downward slope of the road leaving the stone-cutting yards leveled out at the tracks, and from 6:30 to 7:30 in the morning they were always clear, or at least they had been until that day. It had never been a problem, the quarry owner said. The train didn't belong there so late. This was followed by a shrug. The accident was as much fate as anything. No one was to blame. Too sad, he added. The driver was his sister's oldest son. He was twenty-four years old, a member of the family.

He'd probably never needed to slow down before crossing those tracks in the past.

When the truck's brakes failed, the train bulged out on the impact. Seven cars left the tracks and capsized, ripping a stretch of the rails loose with them. The driver was pinned in the collapsing cab between the slabs of onrushing stone and the rail cars. Like the kid at my feet, he was dead instantly.

Walking hand in hand some distance out from the line of the wreckage on the coarse, stony soil, Maya and I counted five dead bodies that morning. I almost expected to hear the sound of the crash still echoing through the air, but the scene was oddly silent.

The Devil Train is not a passenger route. It runs from Guatemala City to the U.S. border and points beyond. Most passengers riding it are on the run, often fleeing a tough situation in a tougher town back home. Others are more upbeat, on their way to a better paying job over the border. The cargo is mainly coffee and sugar, fruits and vegetables, and some inexpensive apparel, most of it destined for U.S. markets. Sometimes a few empty cars on the way to pick up a distant payload are also linked onto the chain. Easy to identify in the rail yard where the train is assembled, they often carry unwanted guests when it leaves. Other migrants precariously ride the roofs of the cars, where access is easy from the ladder next to the brake wheel at the top. Once aboard, they're vulnerable to rain and sun, and worse, to random mishap or its deadly partner, fate.

The seven twisted cars had spilled hundreds of sacks of coffee beans onto the landscape, cases of mangoes, and thousands of pairs of blue and green flip-flops. From the last fractured car a mound of plaid shirts erupted, as random and unrelated as at the used clothing stalls at the San Miguel Tuesday Market. Once darkness settled in, none of this would last long. By daylight, the scene would look like the grounds crew had come through and cleaned up, but for the ruined cars.

As Maya and I walked we saw three empty undamaged upright boxcars with the sliding doors open. These would've held passengers, certainly shaken but still able to run once they hit the sandy ground. Maya's face was dark and brooding.

On impact, it would have been five of those hitch-hikers from the roofs who were killed outright, thrown through the air. No one could tell how many others ran away unharmed or bleeding into the surrounding countryside, since, as we read in the paper later, forty-five cars of the train remained on the tracks undamaged.

This tragedy happened in a part of our horse country that had been serene until that morning, and it was about 9:45 when Maya and I stopped near the compacted body of that young man. Since he was dead we could only commiserate. In his foreshortened posture his face was not visible, but from his clothes I didn't think he was Mexican. He wore a faded blue-gray tee shirt that said *MALDONADO*, and below it, *31*. Below this he had on calf-length cargo pants ragged at the hems. His ruptured backpack had spilled a few items of clothing nearby. Beside them, a comb and a toothbrush wrapped in toilet paper rested on the sandy ground. Flies buzzed on his skin, the only sound.

Maya said, "The ambulances already took away six survivors before you got here this morning." She and I had been together nearly ten years and I don't remember ever seeing that much pain in her face. I put my arm around her shoulders.

Now the police were combing the wrecked freight cars and the surrounding terrain in search of more victims. One of them told us the coroner's van was on its way from Guanajuato. The local medical examiner that normally performed all the autopsies in town worked only as needed. He was a retired eye doctor, and if in some weeks he didn't work at all, he didn't mind. Now he was overwhelmed.

Not far from the dead migrant Maya stood with her eyes half closed under a deep frown. Most Mexicans don't like to get too close to the dead. Her riding helmet was still in place and she was gripping the reins of Martina, her Lusitano mare, in her right hand. The startling wreckage of the train, the sheer numbing violence of it, reminded her, she said, of the big earthquake in Mexico City.

"I was only a baby when that happened, but the debris was piled up in mounds for years in some neighborhoods, although not in ours. Whenever we drove by, my mother used to tell me to keep away from those areas to avoid rats. All the good neighborhoods had been restored first. I was older by the time I realized the damage had favored no one, only the reconstruction had."

Clouds were collecting over the quarry that sliced through the hill to the northeast. This time of year the late afternoon clouds will often work themselves up into a downpour that lasts into early evening. How many migrants were out there now, clustering under the thin groups of mesquite trees, huddling in the shallow arroyos, waiting for us and the police to move on. Many of the rail cars would have some fruit they could take away with them, beyond what had spilled. I stood there shaking my head, making no sense of it. We've seen enough death in the thirteen cases of the Paul Zacher Agency, and it rarely benefits anyone, but this scene expressed a special horror.

It happened along the more distant trails of the very upscale Rancho Aria, where Maya rode Martina four days a week. It was a select environment that offered immunity from tragedies like this, or so you thought once you gained admittance, as Maya and I recently had. Any rider could always be thrown from his mount, of course, but that was his own fault. The Central Americans aboard that train, all young men as far as anyone could see, were merely looking to improve their lives, as were we all in different ways, but they had chosen a tougher course in hopes of making that happen.

Two police officers in navy blue uniforms passed us with clipboards. I stepped back a dozen paces while they scanned the body at my feet, probing the pockets with gloved fingers, checking for identification before moving on. One of them took the victim's left shoe off and probed inside it. Removing the insole, he drew out two U.S. ten-dollar bills and two singles before setting the shoe near the victim's bare feet and slipping the folded bills into the boy's pants pocket. The other shoe had not traveled with him as he soared through the air. Most of these desperate nomads were on the road without documents. If they carried anything precious, they often hid it in their shoes, which can't be picked like pockets.

This far from home, who they were was no longer clear. Another tragedy emerging from the derailment was that their families might never know what happened to them. No money would be flowing back to Guatemala City, San Salvador, or Tegucigalpa in Honduras. Each of the five bodies would be anonymously buried beneath a steel rod ending in a square frame at the top. There a file number would be crudely scrawled on paper under glass. Over time, the sun would bleach that number away, the last meager trace of their identity.

The two officers walked back to the road. This boy had been the last of the five.

The rail accident occurred in July, and we had taken no cases in the Agency since the one we filed as *Angel Face* finished in March. Afterward, I badly needed to step back and gain some perspective. In the last week of that case I had turned forty, nearly lost Maya to another man (quite a formidable one), and come within seconds of dying in a hacienda fire. That was the ascending order of horror I ranked them in. I needed some time to take a hard look at my life. Maya understood my long silences and gave me some space, as I sometimes did for her.

During the weeks following I had painted voluminously, always my salvation, no matter what my state of mind. It may also have been a way of not thinking, since daubing paint onto a canvas does not require the use of any of the analytical parts of the brain, only the creative ones.

While this went on, Maya decided to return to her long dormant high school passion—riding. To me, it was as unexpected as if she had sprouted a third arm, but when she told me about her plan, I could see the inner logic of it in her eyes.

Martina studied the boy's crumpled body for another long moment, wrinkled her flared nostrils and snorted in graphic distaste as she wheeled away, pulling Maya with her. One front hoof pawed the ground. I knew that she detested anything different in her environment, and was ready to move on to less threatening sights. Maya steadied her, and gripping her mane, swung herself up into the English saddle with a modest grunt. She's five-foot six, tall for a Mexican woman, but even for someone with a trim and athletic build, that first stirrup is still awfully high off the ground.

At a walk, she rode beside me back to the stable, about a kilometer along a faint path that wound through the prickly pear cactus and mesquite. I couldn't tell whether the frown on her face was due to the horror of the accident or something else. She had seemed subtly unsettled recently, during a time that was for both of us a readjustment, but she didn't appear ready to talk about it yet.

While riding bloomed into Maya's life again with no warning, I was smoothing out the rough edges of my existence after the *Angel Face* case. Back in March I had been searching for distraction. Maya was drifting too. Our partner Cody had vanished into his third-floor condo on Prologación Aldama the moment March

Madness started. After we finished second-guessing our agency process over a couple of beers or cognacs, he rarely had a lot more to say about a case, although I knew he remained unsettled about *Angel Face*. Some of these cases you have to work through afterward by degrees. Nearly four months later that one was still not fully resolved within all of us.

Immediately following that fire I had found my distraction in a series of therapeutic paintings of vintage rusty cars based on photos I'd taken in junkyards in the U.S. years before. I placed each of them against the ruined facade of one of three local haciendas. It was about textures, rumpled forms, and the color of oxidized metal against ancient stone. They read as sad and nostalgic the way ghost towns do. The best feature of these paintings may have been that they had no connection whatever with my life at the time.

I was unconsciously brooding about earlier days, about symbols of aging and death, images of defeat. Tired of painting worn out tires, I didn't feel the need to go any farther after that trio, even though they sold right away at my gallery in San Miguel. People who know me understand that I follow my eye instead of the trends. Usually I couldn't say what they are. But it was never intended to be a long series, since I wanted to move on, not to linger in the shadows of the past.

Maya, Martina, and I reached the crest of the

low hills behind the grand ranch house and paused. The paddock and ring were laid out further down on the right, with the jumping turf beyond. Past the front gate the highway runs north to Dolores Hidalgo and south to San Miguel. Maya's face was more composed now. Martina glanced at me as if to say, Let's move on, it's time to go home.

For her, home is where the carrots are.

When Maya bought Martina, what I mainly knew about horses was that they could be awfully big, and even if they weren't, you still wanted to watch where they put their feet if they got too close. Even an adolescent pony probably weighs 600 pounds. I had also heard you didn't want to walk directly behind them without giving them a heads up. How could there be anything subtle about an animal that could without warning kick you back over the fence you just walked through?

Hearing that Rancho Aria had a Lusitano mare for sale, one that had been a brood mare for several years and was a bit rusty in her training, brought us out to inspect her. Maya was well aware that she was a bit rusty herself. Within two days we made the deal, and Martina happily remained in her familiar stall among her friends.

When we came around the corner of the owner's house and stopped farther down the slope in front of the paddock, two horses were being brushed and bathed.

Maya took off her gloves and said goodbye to Martina, patting her neck and cheeks. I couldn't help notice the relationship that had grown up between them in less than four months. She found four carrots, and Martina nodded her approval of each of them. A groom named Rodrigo came over, took the reins, and led the horse away. Further down, a woman in the ring was leading her mount through some dressage patterns. Her manner and bearing had a familiar look, but I was too far away to identify her.

Rancho Aria was a scene of great dedication and discipline. No place for beginners, if you weren't serious you didn't get in. I was far from understanding the process or the goals, but Maya was already bringing me along like a young colt newly under saddle. She started naming the horses to me in their stalls, greeting them as we passed. Many knew her. There was Mádrigal himself, the king stud. A sweet-tempered guy, she said, although at sixteen, coming to the end of his best years.

Distracted, I was staring up at the house while she talked about her progress in riding. Although the rancho property was more than 200 acres, the architect had recognized the single finest home site and built on it. Maya had given me only a minimal description of the owners, Max and Phaedra Kingman. This was sketchy because she hadn't yet met either of them. Her characterization of the stalls and exercise pens, the vet care included in boarding, was much more precise, and in her view, unparalleled in this part of México.

A moment later I turned to see a tall Mexican talking to Maya with a familiar grin on his face. Familiar to her, not to me. I had never seen him before. Even dressed in a polo shirt and riding breeches, he reminded me of Zorro, especially in his flashing teeth. He was an attractive man with a widow's peak in his black hair pointing down to a dimple in his chin that had to be a challenge to shave. I could tell it was one he was ready to meet, knowing well the effect he created. His manner suggested that he and Maya went back some distance. High school buddies, I wondered, although he seemed older than her thirty years, closer to my age of forty.

When I stepped into the space between them his smile vanished. Maya introduced me. His name was Raul Sanchez. He had the same family name as Maya.

"Those *ladrones* (thieves) from the train will be all over us before the day is over," he said in clear English, frowning with a wave back into the hills. Obviously, he enjoyed foreign elements in his environment no more than Martina did.

"A few may still be hanging around, but the ones we saw weren't moving very fast," I said.

"Just wait, then. I'm going to put on some extra security in the compound tonight."

He nodded to Maya with a grin and walked off

as if he had other important business to attend to.

"He's the trainer for this entire rancho," she said. "It's an important job and he's very good at what he does."

And at *who* he does, I thought. I saw a subtle arrogance in his bearing that went beyond his job requirements. After Maya's dalliance during the last case, I was reluctant to face that challenge again.

CHAPTER TWO

Until the arrival of Martina, Maya and I had never had even a parakeet as a pet.

"Well, you never know, Paul," she once said to me two or three years ago, but the comment stayed with me. "I could be ready to have a horse again some day. Once you learn to ride, you don't ever lose it."

Despite the shock of the train wreck, this was an engaging time for her, because she'd been so reluctant to give up riding years before. College had been too distant from home and too demanding of her time to allow her to keep up with it, and after she'd gotten her master's degree in history six years later, she went right into researching her book on the early years of San Miguel's revolutionary hero, Ignacio Allende. When we first met and she moved in with me three months later, her oil company executive father was still paying her a monthly allowance to finance her writing.

I knew Maya well enough to sit back and let her settle in at Rancho Aria in her own way, without any input from me, a process I thought of as percolating. Eventually a time would come when she had renewed her skills, settled into her terrain, and established her closest relationships, including the one with Martina and her trainer, and only then would she be ready to bring me aboard. She would proudly display her new world only at the point where it had been assembled and tested.

Within the first month Maya found a nearly new Schleese dressage saddle, gotten it fitted to Martina's short back, and she was launched on the trail to her new life. I didn't think to enquire why this elegant adjustable saddle was for sale after such minimal use, but maybe I should have asked that, given what followed at Rancho Aria. Occasionally an untimely death can bring some high-grade equipment onto the market, the kind of distress sale no one sees coming.

During this period, I painted all day, nearly every day. This continued for more than two months. That didn't bother either of us, since Maya was gone much of the time, framing her new life. As my head began to clear from the *Angel Face* case, I also worked on a series of *plein air* pieces, wondering whether I might also find some painting opportunities at the rancho. Horses are vivid and graceful creatures, full of personality, temperament and soul. The bond they form with humans is worth a close look, and I suspected that to make this relationship work, their riders were not often colorless dullards either. Only an unusual person can get up on a horse that weighs seven times as much as the rider and bring that animal into line using a series of subtle commands, none of which involves much force. Once mastery is established, the relationship often works more like partnership than command.

And by that time I had already learned that anything bearing the word *horse* costs three times as much as the same item without, even if it's only a sack of wood shavings for bedding or a bucket of water.

All the same, I was not surprised that Maya's reentry into the equestrian world was not entirely smooth. Nothing that complex is easy to master, even with her background. Just before the tragic derailment, she came home one day about one o'clock and asked me to fix her a margarita with lunch. She almost never has a drink at that hour, and I never have more than a beer and rarely that.

"OK," I said, expecting to hear some explanation, but she walked away and disappeared upstairs to change out of her half-chaps, boots, and breeches. I brought out the bag of limes and lemons I squeeze and blend for our own version of a margarita.

Ten minutes later we were sitting out in the loggia and Maya still wasn't saying much. Orlando, our long-tailed garden grackle, started to approach her, head cocked to show one hopeful eye, but at five meters out, he sensed an unwelcoming curve to her lips and moved back toward the fountain.

"How's our handsome daughter, Martina, working out?" Surely this sounded neutral enough. As a Lusitano, she has a longish, almost masculine head.

Maya shrugged, a gesture that transcends class, race, or gender in México. "She's coming along. It's going to take a while. Martina has forgotten a lot of what she used to know and so have I. Sometimes these sessions are no more than trying to recover what neither of us remembers. At least I can look up some of it before I go out there. Then I know how to cue her better." She took a sip of her drink and looked off into the garden as if she had no more to say about it.

Maya had already accumulated half a shelf of horse books. I'd removed some of my old painting books to make room—they're both large in format and they only fit on the bottom shelf.

"At least you're both on the same page."

"Mostly." She hardly looked at me during this exchange. I divided the leftovers of last's night's big salad between us.

"Something else on your mind?" I moved the teak bowl down to the end of the table.

"No. You know I don't brood about anything."

"I can see that."

"Partly it's about Raul, the trainer."

"Isn't he good? You said before he was very good."

"He is good. He knows what he's doing. I did say that before. You met him." She didn't go on. I'm often a good judge of character, but a two-minute encounter isn't always enough to develop a focused impression.

Now I wished I had paid more attention to Raul Sanchez on my earlier visits. No ranch that boards other riders' horses, or hires out their own by the hour or for trail rides can function without a trainer. He's in charge of the breeding process in its entire seductive nuance, of raising the resultant foals into a trainable and salable adulthood, of coordinating the periodic care requirements such as vaccinations, worming, shoeing, and feeding. He supervises the maintenance of the physical plant and confronts disciplinary problems as they emerge, not only among the horses, but also among the grooms, who can be a rowdy group, and occasionally, the riders. This trainer is the person whose work the boarders must all relate to, directly or not, every time they visit, and that can be three or four times a week. Maya had been more vocal about some of these other riders than any other part of her Rancho Aria experience.

About a month after starting there, Maya told me that Raul Sanchez was impressed when he discovered he had the same family name as she did. She was not.

I already knew that only about twenty-five family names in México encompass close to 85% of the population. I rarely saw her pull rank within this class structure, although she may have done it more often out of my view. For her, Raul would always be the trainer, and never a stallion, but still a person of strictly defined importance in his own right. He lacked, as she didn't have to tell me, the right bloodlines. Even though he was a prominent person in the local horse world, one commanding the operations of the prestigious rancho, that all stopped when he went home at the end of the day. He did well enough to afford a newish Ford pickup, but she didn't believe he would ever make enough money to think of boarding a quality horse at Aria himself.

"What does all that really mean?" I asked her, when she referred to it again as we ate. Moving a lock of hair off her face, she looked at me as if to enquire why I needed to ask that. She appeared to be considering how much to tell me.

"OK. Raul doesn't know his place. You know how it is here."

This was a serious accusation. Your station in life, as an aspect of class, is like your social address. It fixes you in an exact and unchanging position in society that no amount of money or education can alter. Growing up in Ohio, I held the typical American egalitarian outlook, but Maya had been born into her own status here, and her attitude went with that just as mine matched my Middle America background.

"OK. Is Raul aspiring to a place he doesn't merit? What place would that be?" I was thinking here of Raul using his position as a trainer at an upper class rancho to establish other connections, which are everything here. You can graduate from college with honors and fail to find a job in your field if you're not connected with a firm in advance.

I thought this was insightful, but Maya, after being unusually blunt, added nothing more. I was left to fall back on my own observations, one of which was that Raul might find her more interesting that he ought to. She hadn't said that, but many men found Maya interesting just walking down the street. No problem there, since México is a place where the clear polarity between the sexes is more overt. When a man in a position of power and trust is working with a woman who has more status but less expertise, many degrees of misunderstanding are possible. The grooms that saddled Martina and provided for Maya's needs in the arena all took their orders from Raul.

"Is that all?" I was prodding her a little.

"There is something more."

"Yes?"

"I don't know what it is." She only stared out into the lush hibiscus, not her normal response.

"Some situations are hard to read, but you're a seasoned investigator and the head of the Agency. You're the resource person for cultural nuance and language subtlety, and also the history maven, whenever that comes up."

When she didn't respond, I went on. "You solved that locked room murder in the Oaxaca case, which is every detective's dream." I looked at her with raised eyebrows. It was rare to see her stumped like this; it made me uncomfortable. The Zacher Agency is built like a triangle: if one side weakens, the others risk collapse. Each of us brings our own angle of view.

"I know, but this is too vague. It may not be anything, but I sense an undercurrent at the rancho that I don't understand. It's more than just the other boarders or Raul."

"How does it make you feel?"

She thought for a moment. "It's like when you're in a conversation and you sense that something important is being withheld from you."

"Then why not bring it up yourself?"

"Because I can't think what it is. It's only that I know I'm missing something."

So there it was again, and each time it came up it was closer to demanding an explanation. "Then let me know when it's time for me to pay another visit to Rancho Aria, if only to scout some landscape painting opportunities. I can bring the camera along as a prop. Maybe I'll really take a few pictures. Give me a few days to finish the painting I'm working on now."

"Then Thursday might be good if the light is right, and it has been lately." For the first time in this conversation she looked me directly in the eye, and I could not fail to see the appeal in her face.

But before this scouting visit could happen, the wreck intervened, and Cody and I had gone out to the ranch with a different focus.

CHAPTER THREE

When on that Thursday, the second morning after the derailment, I went back out to the rancho with Maya to get a closer look at her undefined worries about the place, nothing had truly settled down again. By then Raul's warning concerning refugee prowlers from the train had compounded her thinking with a new layer of risk. Unless the escapees from the wreck planned to ride bareback up to the States on a stolen mount, I didn't see a problem for Martina. Raul had said he would add security. I planned to wander around the property to see if I could feel Maya's same sense of unease while I pretended to take some photos.

Gaining entrance was always a ceremony. Rancho Aria has a ramped up drive at the highway that I had passed a hundred times before our horse days without paying it much attention. Above, the clusters of the ranch buildings were grouped going up and down a gentle slope. On the arch over the gates were the words, *Rancho Aria*. A professionally painted wooden sign on one side said, *Home of the Champion, Mádrigal, At Stud*. In smaller letters below, by *Crescendo out of Diva*. While I heard no music from the sign, I could certainly feel the arpeggios of anticipation coursing over Maya as we pulled up to those gates. The place displayed the unstinting refinement of a spread out of *Town & Country*. Perhaps that's why it made me a bit suspicious.

"This is not Connecticut," I said, looking at Maya for a long moment, although I thought the designer of this property might have come from there. Other than on a golf course, I had never seen so much grass in México. I wondered if Rancho Aria was working too hard at making an impression.

A man in livery ran out of the gatehouse and opened the tall gates for us. They were designed as a pair of music sheets, covered with wrought iron triads of notes that scaled the horizontal bars. No improvisation there, I thought. Only one tune was offered. Beyond, we drove up the slope on selected stone pavers that were matched for shape and color.

I parked in the auto corral behind a tall cactus screen. Maya removed her gloves and helmet from the back seat while I fitted the lens on my camera. This kind of trip was nothing new; I often scout locations before I settle on a landscape location to paint. On the way out she hadn't come up with any further suggestions as to what might be troubling her, so I was left to gather my own impressions, something I don't mind. She was usually more forthcoming than she'd been that morning and several evenings before. Part of this was the sobering impact of the wreck, of course. We hadn't stopped talking about it, trying to explain something that should never have happened.

The paddock was quiet, and the groom named Rodrigo told us they'd had no trouble with intruders overnight. Maya went off with him to get Martina saddled while I wandered around the spread. Even far up the slope I could still pick up the faint smell of manure on the breeze and hear the clip of horseshoes on the cobblestones. I wound in varying circles toward the house, following the terrain, checking the façade on all four sides. Only the broad immediate yard was landscaped; the rest remained in its natural state of mesquite and several varieties of cactus. I wasn't thinking about painting, it was only a reconnaissance.

I didn't see many staff people or riders around the upper grounds near the house, aside from two groundskeepers and an assistant with a vague look whose job seemed to be obediently holding bags while the others placed debris and trimmings inside. From the paddock came the whinnying of horses greeting each other and the occasional shouts of the grooms back and forth. When I came back to the front of the house, still finding nothing worrisome, I recognized the woman sitting on the broad porch with an intent look on her face. She was writing rapidly in a spiral notebook.

I had known Amanda Klein for years. She's been a fixture in San Miguel at least as long as I've been here, and I had met her not long after my arrival. As a writer who never promotes her work, it's hard to see how she gets by, at least locally. I've haven't ever seen one of her books for sale in the gift shop at the Library, nor do I see her among the usual literary crowd, not that I run into them much. The San Miguel literati have a distinct presence here, but some of them are a bit standoffish, it seems to me, as if writing is a higher calling than other ways of making a living. Like painting, it's probably not much of a living at all for most people who try it.

A jealous rival of hers once told me privately that Amanda Klein had started out writing women's erotica under an exotic pen name, I think it was Delilah Delaney, when she was still a college English instructor in North Carolina. She had been successful with those books, "bodice rippers," as my informant called them, but over time she'd gotten tired of the genre and moved on. She must have accumulated enough money to coast for some time and didn't have to work very hard anymore, but I believed she did anyway because that was her nature. Whenever I ran into her she was involved in a project. As I sat down next to her on a long rustic bench of weathered mesquite, she pulled a pair of red buds from her ears and gave me a quizzical look.

"Since you asked me, Paul Zacher, I am here working on Max Kingman's autobiography."

Although I hadn't asked, Amanda knew what I did and would naturally expect a question or two. I hadn't yet met Max Kingman, the owner of the ranch, or his wife, Phaedra, and Maya had said little about him other than that he was partially paralyzed from a riding accident many years before. He didn't get down to the paddock much, and few people were invited into the house except for parties now and then. Client parties, she called them, and I knew the Kingmans had one coming up within the next couple of days. We'd been invited, which got Maya hopping with glee when the invitation came. She had been accepted into Equestria, a suburb of Nirvana.

"*Auto*biography?" I said. "Now to me, that suggests..."

She shrugged. "Sure. But a lot of them are ghostwritten. Just because you're famous doesn't mean you're literate, or even very bright, as I've discovered. You'd be surprised. Some actors, for example, can't speak an intelligent word without a script. They mostly have a good memory, which is more important." She spoke in a low tone, even though the row of windows behind us was closed.

Amanda was a slender woman of around fifty,

with curly auburn hair lacking any gray, and a vulnerable complexion she must've worked at keeping out of
the sun. She didn't wear much makeup at that hour of
the morning. The dusting of freckles over her cheek-
bones was pale and sparse. Her lips were thin and had
a look more determined than sensuous. Wearing jeans
with a man's light blue dress shirt in a small size hanging
loose over her waist, she gave the impression of business
casual, but I saw nothing casual about her penetrating
gaze.

"And is Max famous?"

"Maybe in his hometown in Texas, or in his own
mind. I think it's mostly vanity for him, but it pays the
bills for me. You do portraits, so you must know how that
works."

Zzzt! At the center of the porch a hanging bug
zapper fried some hapless passing insect.

"Max detests flies," she said, with a wave, "but
they come with the horses. Sometimes he sits out here
and chuckles as he listens to them sizzle. I think he's still
angry about something from long ago."

"Does he do that often?"

"Just about every day. It's part of his routine."

I tried to visualize this. "How does your process
work here?"

Amanda leaned back into the bench and put her
feet on the rustic planks of the coffee table. Reaching

into her purse, she pulled out a cigarette and lit it. "He tells me about his life, the parts he wants people to see in the book, and I guide the conversation as I tape it. I get paid an hourly rate in monthly installments, which keeps him from dragging it out too long. He still likes to hear himself talk, but he's got the money to indulge that whim if he wants to."

I tried to imagine her role in filtering those recordings. "You must be aware that the content is being twisted in one way or another. In the States they call it spin."

"Absolutely. That part is like talking to anyone, isn't it?" She gave me a careful smile that was not at all shy. "It's like talking to you right now, Paul. No one ever tells me the whole story. It's like you're a friendly guy just stoppin' by here at the rancho for a social call, right? Nothing much going on, you're only takin' a few shots with your camera. I've noticed that Maya is riding now, so that seems natural enough. You're not telling me everything you want from me; but I don't think that awful train wreck and the threat of casual theft by the desperate survivors is all that's on your mind today, is it? Although everybody's thinking about it."

"What do you mean?" My look offered her nothing.

Her face took on a more sober look. "Only that you're not the first person to be wondering what really goes on here at Aria, that's all. Two other people who board here have approached me about it. Both of them had an idea they wouldn't share with me until I gave them something in return."

"And did you?"

"No."

"But you were able to guess what they were thinking?"

"No again, but sometimes I think that's why Max asked me to do this book, as if I could screen him from people's curiosity. That way he can tell people to buy his autobiography if they want to know something about him. He'll say it pulls no punches. Once in print, his story will have more *authority*. Interesting that the word author is buried in that larger word. I rather like that. It makes my job easier." She blew a long plume of smoke over my shoulder.

"You're right about that." With no idea what the other people were looking for, I wanted more from her, so I stared sagely across the yard. "Something has definitely got my antenna up here."

Zzzt!

"You see? Everyone tilts it a little, even you, and others, more than a little. Long ago I stopped thinking my main job was to tell the truth. That was only something I heard in journalism school. You surely don't see it in the media today."

"So the story ends up being partly fiction as you fill in the pieces required for it to make sense. Is Max's narrative making any sense to you yet? Maybe you can manage to have it make sense for me now that you've penetrated my disguise."

"Some of the story reads well just as he tells it." She shrugged and gave me a crinkly smile. "When his narrative doesn't make sense, my job is to find clarity for my reader. That would be someone without your special skills." Her face was like the image on a highway sign; the smile was clear and friendly, the teeth were bright, but her look was only as deep as the paper it was printed on.

This was starting to plug into Maya's undefined anxiety, although I couldn't have said how. As a detective I think about lying all the time, mainly because I get so many lies thrown at me, or slipped under my plate between the covers of an invitation, or pressed quietly into the palm of my hand wrapped in a twenty dollar bill. Max Kingman was apparently engaged in that process with Amanda Klein, and not without the risk of her seeing through him. I wondered whether he grasped how smart she was. That would depend partly on how smart he was, something I couldn't assess until I met him.

"Maybe it's mostly fiction," she went on, her face expressing no judgment about that idea. "Imagine telling your own story as the versatile painter turned detective. You'll admit that's an odd combination, but one that makes for an interesting life, since you now have at least two ways to take serious risks. Talking to me, like everyone, you choose what goes into your narrative; you skip the parts where you stumbled, where you looked bad, if only to yourself. The times when you behaved unfairly. Were you ever ashamed of anything you did? Go back a few years here. For a guy like you, an artist, it probably involved a woman."

Zzzt! I felt like that bug.

"These are the kinds of questions I ask Max, or anyone I interview. Yours could be a book the local gringos would snap up, as well as the folks who are thinking of moving down here. True, it's a niche market, but you're a local personality. I'd shuffle you together with a bunch of people who are a little better known. You could provide the local color part."

I looked at her for a long moment, wondering where she was going with this.

"Half of it is about who you know, and I'll bet that as a detective you've run into some strange people." Amanda closed the notebook and set it on the seat beside her, with the pen clipped onto the cover. For the first time I noticed it was designed to resemble a hypodermic needle. Was it to drug her interviewees, or draw their blood? I made no response as she crushed out the cigarette in a big onyx ashtray that must have weighed twenty pounds.

"You've lived in this town a long time, Paul, and

your moral dilemmas would add some spice and com-
plexity to your life story. Everybody has them, but I don't
suppose they show up in your paintings. Even less, in the
reports you make to your clients for the Agency."

"Maybe in the nudes I paint." I slid my hands
into my pockets and found nothing more to help me
than my keys and two ten-peso coins. Looking down the
grassy slope toward the paddock, the buildings of finely
fitted stone with their ivied walls were prominent and
expressive of a lifestyle I didn't share, or even know. I
couldn't see Maya. "I don't like to go there, Amanda.
You're not tempting me at all." Thinking about the detail
of this, I involuntarily scratched my neck as if a cricket
had crawled up my back and emerged from my collar.
"But now you're reading me, too."

"And this is the part with the fine print, isn't it?
Sometimes I like to work with a magnifying glass."

Or a microscope, I thought. I don't know many
writers, probably with good reason, but I could already
see why I wasn't ever going to ask Amanda Klein to do
my autobiography, or the history of the Agency, even
though I could never do either myself. Writing is a means
of expression that feels far too direct to me. I do a fair
amount of reading, and it seems like the skillful writers
leave a lot of themselves on the page, perhaps more than
they intend or realize. I prefer to smear paint around on
a canvas—it's also a way of getting naked in public, but

fewer people can read beyond the surface detail of it. I needed to move on.

"How is this story being tilted now? By Max, I mean."

"It's all a matter of emphasis. Many things that happen at this rancho tend to evoke his great regret at being disabled so early in his riding career. That turning point informs his life in the same way that other people's lives are defined by their achievements; the important people they met, the awards they received, their photo safari to Africa."

"Now I'm trying to imagine how it would feel if my most defining moment was a failure."

"Exactly. Not being able to resist that twisted story was what persuaded me to take this assignment. You'd think Max would've had a chance to get over it by now."

"Not if he doesn't want to. How old is he?" I knew I'd be running all this past Cody, our staff psychologist, later.

"Sixty-eight."

"So Max has had ample opportunity to clear the boards on this issue, but he must have *chosen* not to."

"Right. He'll take his narrative with him to the grave exactly like he's telling it now. I think his last words will be the same thing he was already saying forty-five years ago."

"If you repeat something to yourself often

enough, long enough, you'll come to believe it. What happened back then? Has he told you any of the detail?"

She gave a long sigh, with a gesture of her hand that must also have expressed his own helplessness as he spoke about it. "He took up jumping late, at twenty-three. I have speculated that it may have been a woman who challenged him to do it, one whose approval meant something to him. Worse, she might have been watching when it happened. I don't know if that would've been his wife of that time or not, because he was already married."

In the farther distance, my painter's eye caught the series of white and red jumps in the arena past the ring, set up in a series and waiting. Did Max often look out there? No one was using them now.

"One day, after three successful jumps at a medium-height bar, he was feeling cocky and had it raised a notch. The horse balked at the last minute and declined the jump, as they say here. Even though the new level was not a huge challenge, Max didn't see that response coming. He was thrown and carried off the field with a severe spinal injury. Ambulance crews weren't as sophisticated then about handling that type of accident. That was forty-five years ago, and if it happened today it might have come out differently."

"What happened to the horse?" That would tell me how much responsibility Max acknowledged for the error.

She fumbled in her purse for another cigarette and lit it with some degree of care. "He had the horse put down three days later."

Zzzt!

Amanda Klein studied my reaction for a moment, as if she were planning to use this as a bombshell phrase in the book, one to end one chapter and hook the reader into the next instead of turning out the light, and she wanted to watch how well it played. I can usually avoid giving much away in an interrogation, which is how I regarded this conversation.

"But this is interesting, and not well known; Mádrigal is a descendent of that stallion," she added, when I said nothing more.

Now I wanted even more to meet Max, because I could easily imagine how much work he had put into developing the legend he'd lived by all those years. As a painter, I work with people's self-generated legends too. They wear them like a suit of clothes, or more often, armor.

Amanda's neutral gray eyes were calm and level with mine. This is the writer's sensibility, I thought—to tell an awkward truth without flinching, to leave the reaction to the reader. I wondered how Max would've told this story off the record, not that he would ever have had this conversation with me.

"Some horse people will tell you the accident happened before he was thrown that day," she said.

"What do you mean by that?"

"I'm not a horsewoman, but riding, as I've learned working on this book for the last few months, is a partnership. I don't only talk to Max. The horse and the rider develop together. When you get a new horse, no matter how good its training and its bloodlines, even a great improvement over the horse you were riding before, it's still a setback in your riding process until your skills and the horse's training come together. Only then can you start to advance at the same pace. When Max was thrown that day, it was because he misjudged something about what he thought he knew, or what the horse knew."

"Did you learn that part from him too? Just being able to acknowledge it sounds like he's made some progress."

Amanda looked away with a long draw on her cigarette and her features darkened. "No, it wasn't from Max that I heard it. That came from Raul."

"Max wouldn't tell you that?"

"I couldn't ask him. Sometimes I try to keep from discovering things he might not want in the book. That doesn't always work. To some degree my job is a tightrope, and I like to keep a little independence for my skills and for myself. It gives me a perspective I can't get anywhere else."

"But Raul wasn't there. I'm sure he wasn't even born when that accident happened."

"Still, he knows horses. They don't change much."

"But does Raul know men?"

"I'm sure he knows them in the saddle, otherwise I couldn't say. Maybe you should ask him. You seem pretty interested in his role here."

I turned away. "He may know women better."

And was Raul's knowledge of horses somehow a threat to Max? "What is Max's relationship with the clients who board their horses here? Has that come up in your discussions?"

"Only in passing. Naturally the income from boarding supports this rancho."

"And beyond that? What is the psychology of it?"

She smiled ironically. "For him, the boarders are always on trial. None of them fully measures up to his standards, least of all to what he could have become himself if his career hadn't been cut short."

"He says that outright?"

"Sometimes he does, but more often it's implicit in the way he speaks about the boarders. There's a weary tone in his voice, as if their efforts are hopeless and only he can see that. In his wheelchair Max has become a connoisseur of riding skills, a judge of everyone he sees in the saddle. His attitude also suggests he takes some pleasure in their shortcomings, although I don't know whether he realizes that. His bedroom overlooks the ring and his remaining strength lies in his authority over this domain. We have sessions there sometimes, when he's seated at his desk looking through the windows over the arena as we talk. The activity below sometimes distracts him as he tells me his story, and he starts to mutter to himself."

"Does he then clarify what he's saying?"

"Not much, except to add things like, 'Look at where her hands are.' Or, 'She needs to hold her shoulders back and stop looking down at the ground so much of the time. That's where she's going to end up herself one of these days.'"

"Does he also make comments like that about the men who ride here?"

"Worse, although there are only three of them, but none of them escapes it."

I've noticed that some older men slowly evolve into cranks, embittered and isolated in their disillusionment. But that happens most often to those who live alone, and have no one to pull them back upright when they start to fall out of line. That element of isolation was certainly not the case with Max, although, who in that household would have the nerve to challenge him on that score if not Phaedra, his wife?

Circling the grounds earlier, I had noticed a more private loggia that overlooked the ring from the northwest corner of the house. Partly screened by plantings, it gave a view toward the paddock below on the extreme left, over the area and the round pen beyond, and even as far as those distant jumps. I now realized it bordered his bedroom. There Max could sit and survey the action, with the single disadvantage that he might also be visible himself from the right angle. I'm sure all the employees would have known to glance up there even if the boarders and trail riders didn't realize he was there.

"How far along have you gotten on this manuscript?"

"We've gotten as far as about eight months ago."

"How is it going, or maybe I should be asking, where does it go from there?"

"It's getting more intense in some ways I can't describe. Although I don't know where it's going next, I can feel something coming. In some of his statements, he seems to be foreshadowing a future event, like you would in fiction. Maybe you don't read any fiction, Paul, but sometimes he's too veiled or self-edited to understand any better than that. As I transcribe it, I make notes on the parts we'll need to go over again for clarification. I know that some of it will be my own embellishment, if only to fill in the blanks. "

"What does that intensity suggest? I'd really like

to see your notes some time."

I had held off asking this, trying to find a more favorable entry point, since she hadn't volunteered everything I needed.

"I can't do that. Sorry. Even if I wanted to, which I don't, some of it is in my own weird shorthand. You wouldn't get it."

Amanda gave me an apparently frank look that expressed nothing as she said this. I didn't ask her to explain further, although it made me wonder whether she played poker in her recreational moments. The most important element was that she worked for Max. She had already shared a lot of information with me, but he was her employer, which implied a relationship that went far beyond any connection she and I had. I realized I had slipped into my investigator's mode without having any strong reason to.

Amanda Klein offered me nothing more. Maya is not a person easily spooked; yet I could also feel her urging me on with this from offstage. She'd become invested in Rancho Aria, and didn't care to have it disrupted.

"I guess I'll have to buy the book when it comes out," I said, thinking we weren't finished with this conversation.

"Don't ask me to autograph your copy. My name won't be on the cover. It never is. The author will be listed as Maximilian Alistair Kingman. I'll get a credit on the acknowledgment page as the editorial assistant, and that's all."

Maximilian, I thought, moving off to find Maya. He was the Austrian upstart, the younger brother of Emperor Franz Josef, who, with French backing, had made himself emperor of México for a few years in the 1860s. He had died before a firing squad in Querétaro. What had Max's parents been thinking?

CHAPTER FOUR
MAYA SANCHEZ

The following morning Maya arrived at Rancho Aria earlier than usual to inspect the condition of the grounds and the paddock before she rode. She wasn't worried about Martina being stolen; the mare was too bulky to be easily sold by anyone who was not in the horse business, and most of her value was in her training and her relationship to a rider she knew. But the idea of a group of destitute Central Americans wandering about those dry hills without resources was cause for concern. The lack of water alone would drive them into settled areas. She felt they were decent people who would soon be starving with no means of moving on to *la linea*, the border up north, a destination they imagined would be salvation.

In contrast, this was the day of the boarders' party, when all the clients and friends of the Rancho Aria would be treated to the gracious Kingman hospitality. She pictured the migrants looking in the windows from their hiding places among the cactus and mesquite. Perhaps Max could be persuaded to donate the leftovers of the barbecue to them. She planned to bring it up if she could find the right moment.

At the gate, the badged and uniformed Carlos Valenzuela saluted her with his usual gusto, and she parked in the auto corral between a white Mercedes SUV and a small red Mercedes coupe. Maya took no special notice of either car, since they both fit her style of upbringing in Mexico City. Part of the appeal of Rancho Aria was that it was an upscale setting that reminded her of an earlier time in her life. She and Paul lived in an ordinary comfortable style without many luxuries. Most of the cars parked before their house on Quebrada weren't worth more than a few months' local wages, and when the owners got out they almost never went into any of the houses on that block. It was only a place to park on their way elsewhere in *centro*.

She left the van carrying a small bag of carrots. Already dressed in her normal buff-colored breeches, with the black half chaps that covered her from her ankles to just below the knees, she wore a closefitting white shirt and carried a dark unlined zip jacket against the chill of the morning. Her hair, black with a touch of henna, was pulled back into a low ponytail. Her helmet, gloves, and crop awaited her in the tack room.

As Maya rounded the curve, the paddock came

into view below. Two people stomped past the fountain in a heated conversation. One was a groom, the other a boarder who furnished most of the excitement. Maya broke into a sprint and reached Martina's stall a moment later. The mare met her at the Dutch door chewing, unconcerned, as if she knew Maya was early and she wanted to finish her breakfast before going to work.

Maya crossed the yard to the opposite bank of stalls and found the tack room door hanging open with a shattered lock. A glance told her that the flimsy hardware had never provided much security. She had never in the past thought to ask herself whether it was enough. With an armed guard at the gate, what more was required? After all, it was the Kingman property. She went into the tack room and studied the scene. The smell of leather and horse defined it as a different world.

Nothing looked out of place. One wall displayed hanging bridles, with helmets on their tree at the corner. Her bridles were both untouched. All the usual saddles were in place on the tiers of braced wooden arms that ran three high up the wall. A few were empty, but that was normal. Rancho Aria was set up to board twenty-four horses, but only three-quarters of the stalls were occupied. With two fingers Maya touched her own Schleese saddle, then studied her hands for a moment. They were fine and small boned, and she took good care of them. She sometimes wondered how Paul could hit a man with his fist, as she knew he had a few times in earlier cases. It was not something she could ever do, although in the previous case she had broken a man's nose by head butting him. Hearing it snap was satisfying enough. It was a sound she would remember for a long time.

She studied the stacked saddle pads for a moment. Since no one was riding that early, the pile looked like it might be low by a few. In the next boarder's space she saw at once that the jumping vest was gone. To an intruder, it may have only looked like a way to keep warm, but it was specially made for jumping and cost around $300.

The latch on her storage box wasn't fastened. She flipped it open. Her new show bridle, still wrapped from the tack store, was gone. Easily portable, it was a $200 item. She felt a wave of outrage sweep over her.

Although Maya had been back to riding for little more than three months, her trips to the rancho had already become her own refuge, personal in the same way she had felt about writing her first book. It was a kind of fortress that offered a serene existence apart from Paul and the Agency, a refined place where finesse reigned in place of confrontation. Feeling this sanctuary violated was more painful than she would've predicted. The only consolation was that the break-in must have been done by poor, desperate people, whose only goal was to survive. She reminded herself that there was no malice in it.

Had Maya pushed this line of thinking further, she would've realized that riding at the rancho and training Martina also offered her something to love other than Paul Zacher, whose near death in the March hacienda fire had left her deeply distraught. Shortly after, she had thought of asking him to close the Agency, but she realized he would never consider doing that after a near defeat. Never one to be put off by a brush with failure, he could only walk away after a triumph.

Maya placed both palms against the rough stucco wall and stood motionless for a moment as anger rushed up within her. Rancho Aria had seemed solid in the same way her father had when she lived at home. Few people could get through that iron front gate. Carlos Valenzuela displayed his gun as an obvious feature on his hip. Unlike the occasional chaos of the Zacher Agency, she had thought Rancho Aria carried no risk of outside violation or intrusion. Now the train wreck had destabilized the lives of everyone in the neighborhood, everyone who boarded there, to say nothing of the migrant travelers who had died, and the families of the unidentified, who would never know. Everyone needs a safe place to go, she thought.

Outside the barred window at the back of the tack room, a weed whip came to life, then quickly died. She turned to see Ivan, the mentally challenged son of the cook. He glanced in at her, but turned away. He was always shy and rarely spoke to any of the boarders unless spoken to first, although she thought he might harbor some fond feelings for her. Maya always made a point of speaking to him when she saw him. She waved at him and turned back to survey her gear.

As she dug through the storage box Maya heard footsteps behind her, and a long shadow passed over her body and her equipment. Someone else had come to check on his tack, but she welcomed no company at that moment. Absorbed in her thoughts, Maya didn't turn around.

"Are you also missing something today?" It was Raul's voice, softly edged with concern, but at once too intimate in tone. Was the trainer asking about her tack losses or her feeling of refuge? His arm came around her shoulders in a comforting way, almost fatherly, until his probing fingers moved along her upper arm, seeking the bare skin below her sleeve.

Involuntarily, her shoulders recoiled, withdrawing into themselves. Without realizing it she shook her head. "I don't know. I don't think so. Some others might have. That jumping vest over there is gone."

Maya couldn't bring herself to tell him about her show bridle. She only wanted Raul to move on, to go back out through that door. Normally when he coached her she was mounted on Martina, aloof, with her hips at the level of his head. Safer. On his feet in the ring, the nearest thing to his hand was her boot and the blunt spurs of German silver. She saw herself kicking up and outward at him, surprised at her sudden anger.

As if sensing her reluctance, Raul lifted his arm from her shoulder. The gesture said his concern was innocent, mere friendliness. Her shoulders began to relax until his hand settled again on her lower back.

"I would like to help you with this," he said. "I can add your loss to our damage report. Of course, I know them all, the police. Some of them are friends of mine. We can't have this going on here. This place is only for us, isn't that true? The right kind of people who belong here."

"What happened to the new security guard?" She didn't turn.

"That bastard fell asleep last night! I won't be paying him. I'm sorry if you lost anything."

His voice dripped sympathy even as his index finger traced the waistband of her panties through her breeches, and then moved lower.

"Take your hands off me!" Even as the words left her mouth, as if on its own volition, Maya's right shoulder launched into Raul's chest with all her weight beneath it. The trainer tilted off-balance on one foot and stumbled backwards into the saddle rack, where the unyielding outstretched brackets caught his upper back and hip before he collapsed to the floor with a painful grunt.

Struggling to sit up, Raul managed a derisive grin that looked more like a grimace. "Then run away, little girl, run away! Why do I need *you*, when I can have any *gringa* here that I want!"

As she turned and rushed out the tack room door, Maya glimpsed the look of alarm on Ivan's face outside the window. Her state of mind was more about rage than satisfaction at any striking back at Raul. She had not left quickly enough to miss his final demeaning comment. At the door Maya saw the French woman who was about to enter and now paused, startled at hearing this exchange. Maya had observed her several times in the ring. She had caught the accent, although they had never spoken, and she knew Paul would've noticed her too. She had that lush kind of presentation that always caught his eye. His hand would unconsciously reach for his brushes and palette when a woman like her appeared. Maya rushed away, throwing her arms into the air, but saying nothing more.

The morning was already a dead loss. Without saying goodbye to Martina, her daily ritual, Maya fled to the parking corral without a word, leaped into the van, and blew out through the gate as Carlos watched her reckless pace with a shocked expression.

Perhaps the party at Casa Kingman that evening,

with many of the most important local riders and ranch owners present, a circle she wished to join, could redeem her mood.

Or perhaps not.

CHAPTER FIVE

Maya returned home more agitated than I'd seen her since the March hacienda fire. She'd been gone barely an hour. As I was walking past the kitchen from the garden, I met her in the *zaguán* in time to see her slam the front door. I came in with my hands palm upward, a question on my face, and a hug waiting in my arms. But she flew past me without a word and fled up the stairs. I had to duck as she lost her grip on her riding crop and it sailed back over my head. By the time I uncovered my eyes, she was gone. If she'd been looking for consolation she would've stayed downstairs.

Answers are not always available at the source of the question, so I pulled the second set of car keys off the baker's rack in the kitchen and found the van about eight spaces down on Quebrada. I could only see this as another layer added to her brooding concern with Rancho Aria. In her state I didn't pause to tell Maya where I was going; if the end of the world had been announced that morning, she wouldn't have noticed.

Three kilometers north of town I slowed down as I turned in, and the Rancho Aria gatekeeper waved me through. I no longer had to pause and say I was Martina's stepdad. The white Mercedes 500 SUV in the parking corral had a familiar look, but this town has more than one of them. Running down to the paddock, I gave it less thought than I should have.

As I slowed on the blacktop path, winding among walls of natural stone formally dressed with manicured vines, I was looking for Raul Sanchez, the next person in line for a probing conversation. But just then a woman rode up from the ring on an elegant and spirited horse, dark reddish brown in color. She rode English saddle with an easy grace and dismounted not far from the fountain, a rectangular basin of polished stone with a single clay vessel in the center that appeared to rest on the surface as water spilled over its brim. Since I was now less agitated myself, I paused to watch her, bringing the artist's eye into the scene. Being a painter, with the way that changes how I see things, was what prompted me to start this Agency years ago.

Emerging from a stall, one of the grooms inclined his head slightly as he presented the woman with a handful of what must have been carrots already cut to half their length. She fed them to the horse one by one, gesturing closely to it, before he led it away. Only then did she decide to turn and catch my eye, although she must have known I was standing there. Still, it was so like her to choose the moment to connect with me on her own terms. It told me where I was on her list of priorities, and my position hadn't changed since the last time I saw her.

I had never known her to wear anything but a dress before, but her breeches and tall riding boots gave her a new athletic grace as she walked towards me. She rode without spurs, perhaps needing none, as in life. Focused and disciplined in this sporting attire, she was still more luscious than lean, and her movements displayed the confidence of knowing that aspect of her appeal. Once again her vivid apricot skin, her broad sensuous lips, and her French cornflower blue eyes spoke to me in the earliest of languages, one that never requires translation.

"Renée Bontemps," I said softly, when she was still ten feet away. She tilted her head and gave me a wry smile.

"Pole Sockaire." No element of surprise altered the steady tone of her voice. "I always knew we would meet sometime again. It was fated to be."

This line made me smile in turn. Either she always felt she was in a movie like *Casablanca* or *Breathless*, or it was only her imperfect English, but the effect was much the same. Renée Bontemps had grown up in Toulouse, where that would be the correct pronunciation of my name. We stood now in a semi-public place, but in the past, in my own *zaguán*, I had heard her private whispers in my ear. I had felt the heat of her mouth on mine and the strong beat of her heart against my ribs. She could never let herself forget how powerful she was. If she had ever experienced a moment of self-doubt, it was too long ago now for anyone to remember, particularly Renée herself.

"I thought you didn't believe in fate." I didn't either, but it was now gaining a marginal acceptance in my mind, since it was Maya who had introduced me to Rancho Aria, where I had never thought to meet Renée again.

"I can make exception when it *mattairs*. You know how flexible I am."

"Only the rumor." She had never been that flexible with me. I hadn't seen Renée in about a year, but suddenly being physically close to her again was worth the wait, even if I hadn't realized I was waiting. She came near enough to place her hands on my shoulders, and planted a neutral kiss on each cheek. I had the odd thought that her horse usually got more from her than that. Perhaps that was appropriate, because she wasn't going to get much from me aside from frank admiration. Pulling off her helmet, she shook out her curly blond and amber hair as if she had suddenly grown aware of her appearance. This is no more than a gesture, I thought.

The last time she'd been unaware of how she looked was probably when she was four years old.

"I should've recognized your Mercedes when I came in."

Renée Bontemps was a woman in her mid twenties who had done well for herself through means that were never clear to me. She now owned a bordello in the upscale Atascadero neighborhood. It was staffed by a string of stunning Central American girls culled from among the desperate immigrants who were the female equivalent of the ruined voyagers from the train wreck.

Starting as a charming but untouchable hostess, she had inherited the business when the owner, Kate Burden, was murdered in a previous case, the one we filed as *The Girl from Veracruz*. Renée had often tried to enroll me as a customer at her elegant establishment. I had always responded that she was the only woman on the premises I found compelling, even though I had never thought her available. Being with Maya, I surely wasn't either. That had never persuaded Renée to ratchet down her appeal. Perhaps she didn't know how.

Still, Renée Bontemps was far more than a one-note samba. Back then I had often glimpsed a shrewd intelligence in our conversations.

"Business must be good," I said. I knew from direct experience how expensive the equestrian lifestyle was. I thought of Martina as the equine equivalent of a

Victorian house restoration in the States—a money pit.

"But did you see my most beautiful *cheval?*" She looked over her shoulder, her arm raised and ready to point, but he was already gone. "His name is Camembert, a son of Mádrigal, by the way, from right on this property! As a colt he was trained by Raul, so he is quite comfortable here on his own turf. Are you having now a case at this rancho, one without me? But how could that be? I hoped I was still dangerous."

Her lips formed a subtle pout; as if this were not the first time I had let her down. This question about a case was one I might have to answer later, I thought. If Raul was preying on the women boarders, how could he resist taking a run at Renée? This suddenly reminded me why I had come out to the rancho.

"Nothing like that, Renée. Maya is riding here. She owns that gray Lusitano mare you may have seen out in the ring. She's usually here at this hour, although she left early today."

"So, yes, I have wondered who she was, but we have not spoken yet. She is very pretty, do you think?"

"I'm sure she knows you."

Fortunately, Maya had never encountered Renée face to face on our earlier case, since we had split up the Agency team, and Maya spent part of her time in Veracruz, although she heard later that some high voltage current was passing between Renée Bontemps and me.

Maya would've noticed her now at the ranch as someone who would catch my eye, but without necessarily making that prior connection if they hadn't been introduced. Certainly her name was familiar to Maya, so this was bound to come up eventually.

"I can only come out here mornings," she said, "when I am off duty."

"Are you taking dressage lessons from Raul Sanchez?"

"Sometimes. Otherwise, I can ride the trails."

"How does he rank as a teacher?" A French version of the Mexican shrug followed, lacking the full range of local nuance, but expressive nonetheless.

"As a trainer Raul is good. But as a man, not so much, I imagine. But you know I am a connoisseur. I see a parade of them at my door every day." I waited without responding, looking into her eyes. "You are wanting to know more about him, Pole, I think?"

"Tell me more of what you know. For example, do you trust him?" I still felt Maya's agitation that morning must in some way have been connected to the trainer.

Renée put her hands on her hips. "Well, I would trust him to be consistent, to be always what he is and no more, no less, once you understand what that means."

"That could mean a variety of things. And is Raul the man he thinks he is?"

Renée grinned broadly, as if I had scored a point. "You will ask me next which man is, right? So now I can make a small list for you." That was not the door I wanted to open with her. The small gap between her two upper front teeth made her smile more intimate. "Of course, I do not know this with him from first hand, contrary to his wishes, but I suspect he is the kind of man that when he comes inside of you, then there is no one left anymore on the outside. Pouf! He is gone like this. He has nothing more to say. To me he lacks substance, do you know?" She snapped her fingers. "You could *peek* up what is left of him like a sheet of gauze and drop him over the side of the bed, where he flutters to the floor without a sound among a group of others like him."

She paused and gave me an ironic smile, as if assessing me in that regard as well. "I always look for much more than that in a man. I'm afraid I must run away again now, but I will see you at the party tonight, I think? I do hope so, Pole. You can be so amusing at times, always trying to think how things work." Her right hand reached out and her fingertips softly raked my cheek.

"I'm sure you'll see me there."

To be occasionally amusing was, of course, my life's goal. I hugged her lightly and watched her move off toward her white Mercedes, the same vehicle I had seen before on an earlier case. I don't know exactly how she acquired it, since it had belonged to the killer who had himself lost his life. Naked but for his expensive loafers, he went down riddled with police bullets on Renée's limestone doorstep. I thought his passing exquisitely expressed the vengeful triumph of the arrogant people in local government he had blackmailed. Still, there are better ways to die than that. The fact that Renée walked away with his Mercedes illustrated, more than anything, how many questions went unanswered below the surface in any typical case. Not that any were typical. We could never define what an average case would look like.

My previous encounters with Renée had all been on agency business, and since I had never seen her with a man, I had no idea about that part of her life. She would've needed someone powerful to keep up with her, perhaps a major business figure from Mexico City, a man who could fly her around in a private plane. She struck me as a woman who easily got what she wanted, and I imagined—I won't say fantasized—that her sexuality was formidable.

Cody had made it clear early on in the Veracruz case that he thought I found Renée far too interesting—as if he didn't—but he always had a way of looking out for Maya's interests when she wasn't around. If I had died in that hacienda fire, Cody would've taken Maya home as her sole support in her grief.

In that last case I'd seen Renée a number of times, and we'd had some frank and revealing conversations. Briefly and early on I had even thought of her as a suspect, and Cody had pushed for that idea even further. Ultimately we concluded she was more a survivor than a schemer.

That was another story. Now here was Renée again, with her undiminished appeal, and I was not put off by the prospect of getting her take on Rancho Aria in a more leisurely encounter. If she had never been fully frank with me in our earlier conversations on the Veracruz case, she still had often been revealing, even if unintentionally, and that would suit me well enough now, as did simply going face to face with her once again.

I don't enjoy interrogating the dull and the ordinary—they're much harder to read because they know so little about themselves. The blurred detail of their lives flies by unexamined, so they can tell you little about it. Give me insightful people, those who understand what happens to them and are willing to invest some time figuring out why. Renée Bontemps illustrated the clear difference between not always offering much, and not having much to offer.

Three stalls down I found Rodrigo, and with a fifty-peso note in my hand, pulled him aside under the roof tiles that shaded both the horses and our conversation.

"Is Señor Sanchez here? I need to speak with him."

"He has gone for the pain medication, *señor.*"

"For the horses."

"No, *señor*, for himself."

"Why would he need that?"

"I did not see it, but someone said he had fallen."

"What horse was he riding?" How could Mádrigal be that hard to handle?

"I believe he was not riding when it happened. That is all I know. I am sorry." He went off on other business.

I stared down into the ring where a young woman was wrapping up her ride. Maya had earlier told me about her and described her in some detail. Her name was Diana Freeman. I took a few steps back into the shade and leaned against one of the posts that supported the tiled overhang.

Diana was a young woman who, according to Maya's account, had spent a lot of time in the saddle since the age of six. Now, as she approached the paddock area, I placed her age at about nineteen or twenty. Dismounted, she was a blonde of medium height, but unlike Renée Bontemps, whose hair was thick and densely curly, mottled with subtle varieties of color, an inviting thicket you could lose your fingers in, Diana's hair was straight, pale gold, and thin in that way it sometimes is for blondes. While it could have been ironed to enhance this effect, it did not invite penetration.

Diana's features were finely chiseled on a similar

scale, as if defined with small tools from a hobby carver's bench, and her eyebrows were almost too pale to set off her eyes. Her lips were also pale, and thin. While there may have been some subtle passion within her, I observed no boldness on display. Some would've thought her attractive, particularly here in the land of passionate black-haired women, but I felt her face looked naked and untested, perhaps awaiting the mark of experience. The problem may have been that I could discover too little to paint in her smooth, cool features. I saw few blues and greens in the shadows of her face, and no warm tones at all.

My impression was that if Raul was interested in Diana, it would be in the way a climber surveys a mountain, simply because it was there, not because conquering it would yield the slightest response beneath his feet.

Observing her from that short distance as she conversed with the grooms, I noticed she had a habit of gesturing with one palm up and outward, with her elbow resting against her rib cage above her hip. Her head was tilted slightly in the same direction. This tended to push the opposite hip out a bit further to compensate. Her manner suggested she was comfortable at Rancho Aria, at least with the grooms, and after watching her interact with her horse after dismounting, I could only believe they were close. Diana's hand again rested lightly on his neck. Some of the animals at the ranch are quite vocal, but this one said little in response, although he held her eye and nodded frequently.

Maya had told me this horse was a spirited Arabian gelding named Pasha. Although not a big horse, he could be a handful because he was not always well behaved in the ring. This would embarrass Diana, and Maya said she had seen a skillful rider's patience struggling at times with Diana's need for perfection in herself. From another conversation, I knew that she had scratched Pasha in warm up at the last minute from several dressage competitions at Tolteca—our local competition venue—and stalked off in a blue funk.

When the groom left with Pasha I walked over and introduced myself. Diana had never heard of me, always a good place to start. "I'm sure you've already met Maya," I added. Behind her, the groom worked on taking off Pasha's saddle as he was tied to the post.

"She's that Mexican woman, right?" I don't know why I was startled to hear this from her. I had known it since I first set eyes on Maya; Mexican was what I was looking for.

"You're right, I went native."

"But I meant it's just that she's the only one riding here. All the other Mexicans are staff."

"I'm sure that's true. It makes her easy to spot, doesn't it?" This close Diana looked painfully young.

"I'm sorry, I didn't mean that she shouldn't be here...I don't know what I meant, OK?" She shrugged.

Neither did I.

"I didn't have a good day."

"Maybe it'll get better now."

She gave me a guarded look. "Now that I'm leaving my horse?"

"I didn't mean it that way."

Maya had also suggested that Pasha's control problems in competition may have mirrored the ones Diana had in her own life, and that the bland but sometimes inconsistent polish of her demeanor may have masked a wild streak she couldn't always restrain, especially, Maya thought, when in competition herself. And are we not all in competition with someone or something?

I wondered whether identifying Diana's perceived rivals at the ranch might throw some light on Maya's vague concerns. Perhaps if I observed her for a while she would do it for me, given that her own control over Pasha was not always perfect.

"Maya is a fan of your horse. He's a beautiful animal. How are things going now in the ring?"

"Well, better. It comes and goes, you know. Some days...like today..." She shook her head.

"I suppose Raul is a big help, as experienced as he is."

Diana gave me a calculating look, but no response beyond a nod. Loosening her up was going to take more than I could come up with at that moment. I hadn't met many of the other boarders yet, and she made me wonder if her veiled presentation was at all typical. Maybe it was only her youth.

"I'll see you at the party tonight," I said, moving away.

Slightly smaller than Mádrigal and his progeny, but similar in color to Renée's horse, Camembert, Pasha was a chestnut with one white stocking and a white blaze on his forehead. He and Diana were well matched; both were handsome animals, neat and trim, and meticulously turned out. Neither of them was very large. His mane was exquisitely and complexly braided. Watching them move in the ring earlier, and now when they parted company, they both appeared to be focused on the thought of when they'd be together again. Deep waters, but with no ripple even in a brisk breeze, I thought, more about Diana than the horse. Other than riding, where was the passion within her? Maybe it would emerge during the party after a glass or two of wine. I wanted to see it if it did.

As the groom took Pasha to his stall I observed Raul standing in the shade of the entrance to one of the empty stalls farther down. I hadn't seen him return to the paddock. He wasn't watching the horse coming in; his choice of animals was Diana while she returned to her small, red Mercedes coupe in the parking corral. While still ten feet away, she beeped the door unlocked, and without looking back, slid onto the glove leather driver's seat, slipped on her designer sunglasses, and drove back to her life in San Miguel.

Raul turned away with a veiled look and stretched his back, rubbing it in two places on the left side.

My business takes me all over this small city in no predictable way, but I had never once come across Diana Freeman on the street. The expat community harbors a variety of social circles, but painters with a practiced eye for solving a murder are not everyone's favorite dinner guest. If the host is not careful, it makes for uncomfortable table talk, because there are some people here who can't leave the subject alone once they know it's your business—even when it's not any of theirs.

CHAPTER SIX

Maya had recovered most of her composure by the time I returned home, announcing that she was going to the party and planned to have a damn good time in spite of all the stupid people around her. Determined to put on a presentable front, her tone invited no discussion, and she didn't ask where I had been.

About two hours before we were due to leave she disappeared into the bedroom and closed the door. This left me thinking she planned several rounds of clothing changes before she made up her mind. At ten before six when we left for the rancho she was dressed in a black knit sleeveless shell and a buff suede fringed wrap skirt. Her arrowhead pendant and silver cuff bracelet were old pieces from the Mexican tourist trade of the 1940s and 50s. She had finished the ensemble with black cowboy boots. I had on a new floral Tommy Bahama silk shirt in one of his less tropical patterns, and black linen slacks I had found no use for during the past year.

In my earlier visits I had been no closer to the house than the front porch during the conversation with Amanda Klein, so I was curious about the interior.

Although having a long porch like this was in itself a salute to the Southwest American style, the rest of the building was neocolonial México, and if you regarded the porch as a way of not entirely relinquishing Texas, it worked all right. The stucco was painted a pale pumpkin tone, with light green *cantera* limestone window and door trim from Guanajuato. The floors and porch roof were covered with reddish clay *barro* tile.

When we first came in, after a small vestibule with a powder room and coatroom, we entered a great room with twenty-foot beamed ceilings. The central block of the house was wider than it was deep, and from both outer edges, it trailed a long wing behind. Together they bracketed a tiled courtyard. The bedroom wing was on the left looking out over the paddock and ring, and the kitchen and service wing was on the right. Behind the house a two-story annex kept the staff at a respectful distance and offered four garage stalls for household vehicles.

Well-worn oriental rugs covered much of the floor. The feeling was of old, informal, but high quality family furniture that had found its way down from Texas. The folds and crevices in the upholstery probably concealed the dust of history: brass buttons from

World War I uniforms, five-dollar gold pieces, jet black hat pins and Indian head pennies. At least thirty people were already present when we arrived, and two more couples were behind us. Inside, few were seated. The atmosphere sparkled with excitement and anticipation.

This was the annual boarder appreciation barbecue thrown by Max Kingman and Phaedra Montgomery. It looked like a dressy affair in an informal way, with the Texas overtones overlaid on the relaxed good vibrations of San Miguel hospitality. The celebratory feeling was not visibly marred by the whisper going around— the first thing we heard—that the pantry storage room behind the kitchen had been broken into the night before. No one knew in detail what had been stolen. While Max and Phaedra were said to have a *bodega* for their personal valuables in the wall between their bedrooms that had not been bothered, it seemed that food had been the principal target.

The weather was perfect for July, the midpoint of the rainy season. Up in the hills beyond the property a few high shredded clouds hung about trying without success to congeal into a cluster, but nothing more threatening was in view. It was a moderately warm evening with no wind. Maya and I circulated to get a feel for the house. The terraced area between the two wings in back had been roofed with canvas, and the barbecue was set up in the yard beyond. Next to it was a tent serving as a kitchen annex. This way the guests, who would be seated later at eight circular tables under the canvas, could be served without traffic going through the great room.

Inside, everyone seemed to know each other. In this horsey group I was instantly out of my element, as I knew I would be, but as a painter, to some degree I'm always doing a little promotion, so that didn't matter. Maybe I could uncover some demand for a few horse portraits. Maya began to point out people whose names she had mentioned to me before. Near the entry were the Camarenas, who owned a property just north of the ancient pilgrimage village of Atotonilco, not far up the road. He was an equine vet and she was a small animal vet. Their spread had been on our list of possible places to board her future horse until Maya saw Rancho Aria when she came for the first time to look at Martina. I wondered whether she was now reconsidering that choice.

My growing sense of Rancho Aria was that it was like a beautiful woman, well turned out, one who worked at concealing her past and was also somewhat vague about what she did for a living.

Studying the crowd, my attention was captured as well by the art. The tall ceiling of the great room provided for impressive art spaces directly below, and eight large paintings were hung that were obviously by the same artist. The theme was Art Deco high life, a social series of exotic houses where 1920s and 1930s cars lurked outside like sleek animals among the tall Roman cypress, flanked by elegant women in flapper dresses and marcelled hair, and tuxedoed men worthy of magazine covers, martini glasses in hand. The color designs were subtle and compelling, with a lot of gray and magenta, sable and olive, set off by a blush of peach and pale turquoise, with silvery highlights. I wondered if the room had been designed around this collection. In the final picture of the series, standing next to a Duesenberg, a striking young man casually held the reins of an elegant horse.

"A Dutch Warmblood," Maya said, with a nod. The man wore the shadbelly tailcoat of a dressage rider, and his look of innate comfort and belonging within that group said this was his family's turf. His blond hair was parted in the middle, just as a strong cleft parted his square chin. His straight nose spoke to his strength and determination, even as his bearing was graceful and gestural. The most stunning feature was his piercing blue eyes as he stared back at the viewer. I studied the signature on that painting. It was J. C. Leyendecker, a name that meant nothing to me.

The interaction of these textures and colors, the seasoned furniture speaking of old comfort and long tradition, made me think that Max and Phaedra must be interesting people descended from a long line of other interesting people. The message was clear. Yes, we are Texas, it said, and yes, we are horses; we are ranches and banking and beyond, but our old moneyed roots lie deep in the East.

At that moment a server came up with wine in two colors and Maya and I each took a glass of red.

"Your look has caught the tone perfectly tonight," I said to her. "I hope you can let go and enjoy yourself." She was starting to relax, but I knew that being determined to have a good time didn't always make it happen. Usually it only makes you drink too much.

On the other side of the terrace I caught sight of two other ranch owners I already knew, and three or four others prominent in the expat community that I hadn't thought of as riders. The conversation was animated and personal as I wandered through this group that had now grown to about forty people. Maya and I had separated soon after getting our drinks, since I only speak "horse" with a mild stutter and a strong painter's accent, but she was already learning the more advanced vocabulary of that most specialized and nuanced language.

"I swear she drugged him in that last competition," I heard someone say as I walked past, slowing slightly. "It was either that or scratch him again. You *know* how she hates to lose."

"But I've never seen her have any fun when she rides," the man said, taking a long pull at his drink. I thought this sounded harsh. Were they talking about Diana?

"Drake hates the water more than anything," someone else said in a confidential tone three steps on, turning her back on the man himself, barely fifteen feet away. "You'll never see him ford even the tiniest stream on one of his trail rides. I think it's because he can't swim, and he's not sure whether his horse can, either, old Buck." The surrounding chatter would've kept Drake from hearing this.

From an earlier conversation in the paddock near the time when Maya first started boarding, where he had probed me about doing his portrait for a reduced fee, ("It'll be good publicity for you. Everybody knows me here and they'll all look to see who painted it.") I had learned that Drake Wilson was a successful businessman of about fifty-five, with an academic background in archaeology in the States. Oddly, he volunteered to me that he had never been on a field trip after college, as if by graduating he'd done his duty and moved on.

He had minored in Spanish, and wanted to carry on the conversation that way. Although his command of syntax and his vocabulary were excellent, to my ear his accent had never gelled. For this party he wore a buckskin jacket with fringes running down the sleeves. It was as if he was trying to make a statement, but what was it? Over a well-tanned face, his iron-gray hair ended in a widow's peak, a feature I associate either with lounge act piano players or vampires. Or with Raul, as I'd noticed earlier. I was pretty sure Drake was neither, although the evening was still young, and later the moon would start to define its presence through the high back windows of the house. He might bloom then in unexpected ways.

Maya, who had mastered a sophomore level of rancho gossip not long after her arrival, also told me Drake Wilson had been divorced by his wife two years after his arrival in San Miguel. He now ran a tour company that brought visitors out to our minor league pyramid and a few other historic sites in our state, like the grand ruined hacienda of Jaral de Berrio, about an hour and a half to the north. His business slogan was, *Guanajuato up close and personal, with an insider's eye to the past.*

Wilson was popular with tourists, but not so much with locals, although he had a prominent profile from a lot of advertising. If you searched San Miguel on the Internet, you soon found him tapping on your shoulder through an ad in the margins. Despite the fact that he thought his commonplace statements were almost profound, it was still difficult to dislike him, even though I hadn't stopped trying.

After that first conversation in the paddock, I concluded that he had mastered one important thing: if you want to be interesting in talking to people, you need to express some curiosity about the other person's lifestyle and interests. Drake did this well, although he may not have had much to draw on himself.

Two women in cocktail dresses passed. This was not the normal San Miguel party attire; I figured they must be northern visitors who knew one of the boarders. "That's exactly why he had a vasectomy," one said, with a knowing look. "He didn't want to be a two-family parent." The other giggled.

Maya also told me that Drake's horse, Buck, was steady, plodding and utterly bombproof; a regular gelded equine good fellow, one that made the other riders wonder how polished a horseman Drake really was. Riding Buck, Maya said, you could fire a howitzer one handed from the saddle and the horse would barely notice. He was apparently named for something he'd never done. Maya felt this may have been because Buck was five years older than Drake thought he was, and partially deaf. Drake only rode him a couple days a week, which was good, since Buck appeared to need a lot of rest between outings.

"And I said to him, 'If you pinch me like that again, you had better mean it.'"

"Well, he usually means it at the time, it's only that later he doesn't recall what he did, or why."

I whirled around too late to see which woman said this. I expected to see Raul lurking nearby, but he was not in view.

Within the crowd my meandering glance fastened on Renée Bontemps, wearing one of her sundresses—spaghetti straps with a tight bodice, a touch of broad cleavage, and a loose skirt that ended about four inches above her golden knees. As the fashion magazines will tell you, skin is not just for the beach; it's versatile enough to work well as eveningwear too.

Renée's jewelry was more upscale than I'd seen before, and from where I stood, the pendant on her neck appeared to be a scarab of solid gold. I'd have to get closer to be certain, which was not likely that night, but I couldn't imagine her wearing anything gold that wasn't solid. She had turned to respond to Drake Wilson, and her body language said she found him more boring than bracing. Although she faced him at eye level, her torso was slightly turned away as if she had only paused for a moment to make a response in passing, since she was on a more important errand. I wondered who she might be connecting with. After studying her for another lingering moment, I moved on.

"As usual, it was a foolish choice of sires," a forty-ish man with a gleaming shaved head and perfect teeth remarked to his boyish companion, who closely resembled Robin in the *Batman* movies, although he wasn't dressed that way. Perhaps he would be later. "Bad advice. That bloodline was always short on wind. Now they'll spend a mint on training, and he'll still fail in the stretch in his first race. He also lacks enthusiasm. Some might call it spirit."

"No one could ever say that of you, Charles," the boy responded, looking into the crowd with the manner of having come up with the right thing at the right time.

I drifted on again, trying to connect names with faces.

"Of course, I really *love* the idea of a woman president. I just wish a candidate was out there I could stomach."

"You're thinking Candace Bergen?"

"Oh, no. Too Hollywood, and too television, even though she's got the dynasty part right. You remember her dad, of course, always with his dummy."

Or, ten feet on, "It's the humidity. There's been too much rain this summer and it's never dried out. I know we can fix that hoof problem with copper sulfate."

"Some of the grooms use Venice turpentine. It works just as well. Of course, Max never would allow that. It has to have the right label or he wouldn't touch it."

"Max has never fully gotten over Molly Ringwald."

"I wonder if *she* has the right label?"

"Molly or Phaedra? I'm sure Phaedra's label is quite proper, even if the rest is somewhat iffy. I always like to walk past and guess what her latest procedure has been."

I glimpsed Maya moving through the crowd at the far end of the room with a more determined step than I had. At some distance, Raul stared after her with both palms extended. His movements seemed a bit tentative, resting his weight more on his right foot than the other. She ignored him with the stiffness of a bristle brush.

"But Raul Sanchez is *her* stallion, don't you think?"

"Yes, but who else's as well?"

"You have a dirty mind."

The man shrugged. "Phaedra tells me everything."

"And nothing. That's what she wants you to think. She was an actress, remember? You don't lose it. The only time anyone ever encounters the word fidelity in this social set is when they open the monthly statement from their trust fund."

I had known as we walked in that this was not precisely my crowd, but now I began to wonder if the riding group here was a bit incestuous. Had everyone long known each other's dark secrets from direct experience? San Miguel itself, the expat community, and the equestrians, were all relatively small groups. I had noticed people glancing at me as I passed in the crowd, wondering who I might be and how I'd gotten through the gate.

About half an hour after we arrived, a young Mexican in house livery, a white jacket with black slacks, began taking prompted shots of people deep in conversation. Perhaps readers would later see photos of this exclusive gathering in *Town & Country* magazine. More likely it would be in *Atención*, our local bilingual weekly. Surprisingly, I didn't see any sign of Max. Did he have an elite group of fans tucked away in a more intimate venue? Riding must have hierarchies here just as many other things did.

Standing in the corner was Diana Freeman in the company of a tall blond man of nearly forty, almost twice her age. I didn't recognize him, although his expression of self-importance suggested that I should have. He was wearing what I would call a shooting jacket in a nubby tweed. It had a suede leather pad mounted on the front of the right shoulder and was belted below like a Norfolk jacket. I guess if you were not a rider, any sporting gear could be a valid credential at this party. Had I known that earlier when I was dressing, I would've worn my old bowling shoes to give me some sportsman status so I could fit in better.

Near the patio wall, Maya was still talking horses with people who really understood the subject. I was surprised to see her so much in her element after less than four months back in the saddle. I was starting to pick up some of that language, the nouns more than the verbs, but not fast enough to have a real conversation in this group. Without Maya telling me, I had realized early on that it would be a mistake to make any reference to Roy Rogers or Dale Evans. I saw no other painters. They would've looked utterly sportless here, as I did. Painters are rarely perceived to be great athletes, since the muscles of their eyes don't ever ripple as they work.

When the crowd shifted a bit, I spotted Raul Sanchez again, now trying to talk with Diana Freeman. Her tall date was missing, and she edged away from Raul with an irritated look on her face. His wolfish grin suggested that he knew her weaknesses. Her none-too-subtle withdrawal suggested she knew his.

I understood how that could be true. If you look at all women the same, you will not see a single one of them.

Behind them Drake Wilson bent toward a Mexican woman to whisper in her ear. She was one of the few non-gringo guests here. One of his hands gripped a drink and the other gripped hers. The woman's expression hinted that she had hit the big time. His did too. I wondered whether they were both wrong, or both right. Were their grins about being together, or merely being at this party?

She was an attractive woman close to thirty, tall with her dark hair clipped back on both sides with a mother of pearl comb, and falling to about ten inches below her shoulders. I put her height at about five-foot-eight. She wore an elegant pair of slacks that draped nicely on her long legs. When she turned, her eyes caught mine and she gave me a slight smile that dissolved into something else I couldn't read before she quickly looked away. In that instant I had noticed her mouth was soft and expressive, and her eyes spoke of a dynamic emotional life.

During my slow circuit of the room, a male tuna band in Renaissance costumes had drifted in as I was scanning the crowd. They had nothing to do with fish, and I hadn't seen so much purple velvet or that many black tights in a while. All nine of the members were now staged against one long wall in the great room, and at three hits on the tambourine they began to play traditional songs from old Spain, rather than old México. The tenor had a standout voice. This was *Tuna Provinciana*, a group I had heard before, and I thought their music would elevate the gossipy tone of the party. Unfortunately, their efforts only drove the volume level of the conversation higher. As I moved on, I found myself slightly surprised that I hadn't found a single person to connect with. If I had seen any of the guests scanning the paintings with awe, I would've sidled up to them for a chat.

In the center of the crowd Phaedra Montgomery raised her hand for local silence in the group of three young men who faced her. Beyond this circle, the general volume did not diminish. She possessed a statuesque grace in a draped black chiffon shell and matching wide leg pants. It was clear that she had not gone Western for this party.

Amanda Klein slipped past me to get closer to the music as I moved nearer to the lady of the house. When Phaedra spoke, her voice expressed the self-conscious allure of Vivien Leigh, yet with a touch more class and several degrees less neediness. The role she was playing that night was that of the seasoned theater star accepting the admiration of her fans. I moved on, since the content seemed scripted. I always prefer improvisation.

The mariachis were not bad, but they soon launched on a string of standard melodies I'd heard too many times, so I left the crowd and stepped outside to the long porch in front. I hadn't seen Maya for a while. Down the gentle slope, someone walking off toward the paddock but off the blacktop path, his boots muted by the grass, caught my attention, but the light was too dim to make out who it was. Reminding myself to relax, that I had nothing to prove that night, I turned to discover Renée Bontemps standing three feet away and looking into my eyes. She set her wine glass down on a table at the end of the *equipal* sofa. As good as she looked, even in that dim light, I now wanted her take on the group inside more than anything else.

"Tell me about what happens at this rancho, Renée. I think it's not only about riding." I moved closer as if to not be overheard, or only to be nearer to her. No one else was around, and the music inside prevented any others from overhearing us. From six inches away she gave off a warm, subtle scent that did not come from a bottle, but from her physical presence. The feathery caress of her breath on my face made me want to draw her against me.

"So, what do you want to know, Pole? You are the detective, I believe. Maybe it is you who should be telling Renée what goes on here. I can see you have some ideas about this already. I would like to know also." We were so close I heard the edges of the words forming on her lips.

Even though the light was failing, I could still clearly see her eyes. I shook my head. "For me it's too early in this game, and you know all about games." I took a sip of my wine, which I had hardly touched. "Do you deliver fantasy at your establishment?"

A tiny shrug. "If that's what is required. Often it is, do you know?"

"And you don't charge extra for that?"

"No, up front we charge enough to cover it. I don't like to *neeckle* and dime our clients."

"And what are those fantasies?"

For a long moment she looked at me without blinking as if considering what mine might be, and whether she had earned a role in them.

Zzzt! Zzzt! I wondered whether there wasn't a switch on that damn thing, but I wasn't about to put my hands on it to find out.

She moved away from the sound, farther from the entry, into deeper shadow. I followed. "They are often about being a *beeggair,* a more powerful and exciting man than they were when they came through the door. We provide a portal into a different kind of life, one where for half an hour everything goes your way for a change. No one questions you, and no one pushes back. You are in control."

"Mastery of your companion, and her submission to a greater force?"

"Yes, usually, but sometimes also it can be with a tiny bit of pain. That requires a good tip."

"That's what we have here at the rancho, don't you think? You must see that in the ring."

Renée didn't answer for a moment. A sudden movement down at the paddock silenced us, although no one there could have heard our conversation. Finally a light went out, followed by the sound of the tack room door firmly closing. I couldn't see who walked out toward the front gate, but the person was not a party guest, since he did not go by way of the parking corral. The path avoided the house and was not fully visible behind the landscaping. It was not Raul; he was at the party inside stalking Diana, unless he'd moved on to another prospect. I felt like something was happening that I didn't understand. Without knowing why, I made a mental note of the scene for later. It was more likely that I was just too jittery.

"Mastery, you are thinking," she said after a long moment. "The rider is always in control, calling the shots."

"Yes, if he can." I suddenly thought of Max, going over the jump alone when the horse refused it. "So if this rancho is the horse, then who is the rider?"

"Well, I do know who would like to be, and possibly is some of the time. You already know his name."

"Raul Sanchez."

Renée didn't respond. She didn't shrug or nod, but only looked back at me on the darkened porch. I leaned closer to her face, where I could mainly see her teeth and her eyes. I placed my hand lightly on her bare shoulder and my voice dropped.

"Tell me more. I helped you once, two cases ago. You were the only winner then; I don't know if you ever knew that. Four people died in that drama, one of them on your front step, but you only moved ahead. Now you are here."

"And where am I then?" Her voice was a coarse whisper as she shifted her weight from one foot to the other before she turned her head away from me. I heard her shoes on the tiles. "Now I have become like the Mexicans, you know? I don't like to get involved so much. I have my business to run, and, of course, we are known to be discreet. Without that, why…"

"But you *are* involved. Staying clear of whatever is going on here is only an illusion. Hiding your head in the sand doesn't mean no one can see you." Of course, I knew nothing but Maya's impressions and the vibe I was getting from the place, the insights of Amanda Klein, and now, from Renée Bontemps on that porch. Diana had given me nothing. Perhaps she had nothing to give.

"Tell me what you know." Without intending to, I seized Renée's wrist. She did not resist, and her skin was cool on my palm. Clearly she was less excited than I was, probably her normal position with almost any man she met.

She turned to face me from inches away. Placing her other palm on my cheek only drew me closer. Her mouth opened slightly and her lips brushed mine with an electric charge.

"Talk to Phaedra," she said in a whisper. "That is where it began." She slipped her wrist out of my grip as she spun around and went back to the party. As she passed through the door, the glow from the carriage lamps clutched at her vagabond curls and lit the swirl of her skirt.

Zzzt!

I stood there in silence for a while, wondering if horses functioned as amplifiers of human emotion, boosting the scale of everything that went on around them. In college I had worked one summer as a switch-man for a railroad in a switchyard not far from my home-town in Ohio. My main memory of it is that everyone in that yard yelled and cursed all the time, as if the shear mass of the huge machines we were muscling around as we made up trains demanded a higher volume of expression. A single mistake and you could demolish an entire freight car with all its contents. Naturally, for coupling the air hoses together between the cars, we received hazard pay of $2.14 a day.

There is no hazard pay in the job I have now, and sometimes no pay at all. I'd had this same thought the moment I saw the derailed cars.

As I stood there thinking about this, someone else came through the door, the one that Renée had told me about.

CHAPTER SEVEN

I t's so dark out here now," said Phaedra Montgomery, or Mrs. Max as some called her. "Shall I put more lights on? I saw Renée Bontemps come back in a moment ago, in rather an unseemly rush, I thought. I hope you two parted without rancor?"

"Rancor? How could anyone feel rancor towards Renée?"

"I am so very pleased you were able to come," she said, ignoring my question as she seized my hand between hers and introduced herself. "But you're quite alone out here now. I don't care to see that in my guests. Is everything all right this evening?" The same question I wanted to ask her.

Our hostess was an imposing woman with a regal bearing she might have copied from the Queen of England, but without that sovereign's recent decline in vigor. I had observed Phaedra earlier in the evening as I walked through the crowd. At a hair over six feet in height, I was only about two inches taller than she was.

My first impression of her was that she was an astute observer, a skill I always cultivate for myself, in both my careers. I knew this by watching the movement of her eyes. When she spoke, her accent was elegant upper class English, and her hair was burnished silver by careful choice. If gray always looked that good people would want it as a fashion choice. In the better light inside, I had tried to guess her age, but judging from the subtly uncoordinated tension among her features, instead I realized that she had probably had the benefit of more reconstruction than Colonial Williamsburg.

She reached over and switched on a lamp at the end of the sofa. Instantly the zapper leaped to life again. *Zzzt!*

"Oh, don't mind that," she said.

"I can imagine the tray under it filling up with a heap of withered bodies."

"But we have staff for that. Besides, Max likes it. It entertains him."

Phaedra's eyes were uncommonly bright, like those of an unappreciated high school girl who hadn't expected you to ask her to the prom. They were also slightly more open than perfect vision required, even in the low light of the porch. Although it was an ingénue look designed by a plastic surgeon, the penetrating intelligence behind it made me think that little got past her. Perhaps because of it, she also seemed somewhat startled in her attitude, as if you had implied something you didn't fully intend in a harmless statement or remark about her wallpaper or china. A furtive, half-closed look would've been beyond her capability. I wondered how she slept. Did she search the blank ceiling, shuttered in darkness, still unable to close her eyes? She must wear an eye mask to bed.

Exposed in its upper stories, her broad bosom was like a frontal assault. Even in that chancy light I could see it had surrendered none of its thrust and parry over the years. Who knew what surgical tugs and tiebacks were involved in that? What ligaments from goat legs and tendons from raptor talons had been commandeered and bonded to some inner structure? Even her neck was tight and smooth. It gave nothing much away about her age or anything else, nor did Phaedra herself.

"I'm very pleased to be invited," I said. "Renée was not upset; she only thought of something she needed to do. I've known her for a while, since we met on a case last year." I could think of absolutely no way to bring the conversation around to Raul, nor was I certain anymore that I wanted to.

"Case? I hope you're not working tonight."

"Don't worry, I'm on nobody's payroll." While true, this did not address her question.

"I must tell you that Max has been watching Maya closely." She leaned toward me slightly.

Max too?

"She is, as he says, a woman who has returned to her own essential element after years of being lost trying to please other people."

Lost as in writing her own book on Ignacio Allende, our hometown hero of the War of Independence? Lost as in seeing it translated and published in two languages? What was Max seeing that I'd missed? Just how astute a comment was this?

Even as Phaedra's voice had projected great power and flexibility inside, her current whisper could've compelled the attention of the back row. Maya had told me she spent her acting career in West End London, playing women of a certain class and refinement, and had married Max fifteen years earlier in a whirlwind courtship—these were Phaedra's own words, Maya said.

The idea of Max and the word *whirlwind* in the same sentence left me puzzled. I like to judge people by what they do, rather than how they present themselves, but what they offer for openers can still be revealing. Yet I tried without success to square Phaedra's statement with what Amanda Klein said Max's typically negative comments about the boarders were.

"Your husband is very perceptive." About some things, perhaps, but not so much about Maya.

Phaedra Montgomery waved this away with a gesture that showcased the enormous diamond and platinum ring on her left hand.

"Of course. He has had time to observe, and even more time to think about the human condition."

Zzzt!

Phaedra's manner was cordial, if slightly formal. This gathering was a business affair, and I felt she was making a visible effort to relate to me, where a more truly gracious person would've connected without letting me see her work at it. I tried to imagine painting her portrait. How would I pose someone who was always posing? The task would be to persuade her not to pose, even as she posed. The best I would probably get was a woman who was posing as a woman who was not posing. Painting can be a shell game—what to emphasize, what to downplay, what to simulate or what to hide—but that's one aspect of it I don't mind. Maybe if I asked for her autograph it would loosen her up. She would then better know how to look down at me.

"I suppose part of Maya becoming so engaged is mainly due to the efforts of Raul. She told me he's invested a lot of time and close attention in her training." After Renée's comment about Phaedra holding the key, about the problem having begun with her, I watched her reaction.

A subtle stiffening of those of her features that remained flexible suggested I had gone down the wrong trail. That was all. I was suddenly reminded of a tune from many years back, *Will You Still Love Me Tomorrow?* Had Raul dumped her? I saw no way to introduce the subject of Raul and Phaedra together.

At her gesture, we rejoined the party. She turned to watch the performance of one of the servers passing out hors d'oeuvres. His tray was a few degrees off true level as he bent over, and she swooped down on him with a gentle swat that didn't connect, while muttering a comment I didn't catch. My moment was gone, and I suspect she didn't regret its flight. Her manner said that a hostess's job is never done until the last guest is out the door and the last platter is in the drainer at the sink.

Having been dispensed with by Phaedra, I took that opportunity to move on to the ringmaster of this equine circus, Max Kingman himself. A man well named, or was he? Was he truly in control of what went on at Rancho Aria? In trying to describe a person it helps to see him moving about, working a crowd, and especially, interacting with people one on one. Private expressions always reveal more than public poses.

When I'm starting a portrait I encourage the subject to chat about the coming artistic process, which few know anything about, and move around as I try to find the right pose while I mix some colors. If he is shy or graceful, confident or clumsy, this interaction will tell me within a few minutes what kind of person I'm looking at. If he has nothing to say, I won't be able to know what he thinks, or what he wants me to think he thinks. But shy people rarely sign up for this process.

Knowing what he wants me to think of him is always useful as I paint, even if the impression he wants to give is not true, because knowing the falsehood he prefers still tells me something about him. So this kind of mobility is important. But if you are looking at a man lying down, you cannot describe his height, or the way he might dominate a conversation in a group. He is like a rolled up rug; he will have no *presence*. His personality is turned inward, switched off. But seeing him interact with others reveals his need for dominance or his receptiveness to other people's importance. This was the problem with Max. I had quickly realized that a wheelchair could function as a mask as well as a means of moving about.

With a new glass of red wine in my hand, a Malbec from Argentina, I stood at the French doors opening to the broad terrace, now shaded from the brightening stars. The hosts knew that you cannot trust a July evening here. At a large table in the center of eight others sat Max Kingman with a variety of boarders and guests. In the middle was an ice sculpture of a horse's head, probably Mádrigal. My viewpoint was too distant to make out their conversation, but I wanted to watch his body language.

Of course, we are all faced with many kinds of masks. The white lab coat your physician wears as he examines you is one. It's an impersonal façade that speaks of hygiene and authority behind which he can deliver your death sentence in a detached and professional way. The cop's urban riot combat uniform and the blank glare of his bronze sunglasses, behind which he can club you to the pavement, more or less anonymously, act the same way. The palette and brushes I hold in my hands when I'm working on a canvas, the structural mass of the easel I sit behind; these are all parts of the painter's mask. They move me back a few steps in this otherwise intimate encounter. They make me less approachable. Don't talk to me now, they say, as I mix some colors. It all makes you feel frozen in place as you pose. If you move I might get it wrong.

The horse that equestrians choose to ride might be one of their masks too, projecting a statement about their personality and the kind of presentation they favor. I thought of Diana Freeman, and Renée, with her horse, Camembert. The money they spend on their mounts is part of it. Clearly, another aspect is that when they're in the saddle, their heads are two or three feet higher than anyone else's on the ground. They so easily look down on people who're not also mounted. This was a major part of the *conquistadores'* advantage when they first met the Aztecs, who had never seen horses before. It was mainly the combined godlike mass of horse and rider together that was so formidable.

Thinking of his confidence, his current mastery of an audience, I wondered what Max's demeanor had been when he was still riding. And conversely, how did he pull this off now, since in his wheelchair he was perpetually two feet shorter than anyone near him? His head always matched the height of an eight-year-old. This was an inversion of status few people could have undergone without some major psychological adjustment. I wasn't sure Max was immune. Amanda Klein had given me some hints, but I wanted more.

Despite what he conveyed to Amanda about his bad script, he had chosen not to act the part of the tragic hero in his own life. Instead, ongoing equestrian mastery was his game, even if performed from the sidelines. In this new role, although an apparently passive one, he'd been able to soar above the other actors, because their insight about equestrian skills could never match his. Amanda's ability to read between the lines was something I couldn't assess, but I wasn't inclined to underestimate it.

As I watched this scene, on the surface Max's manner suggested he had borne up well with the severe deal fate had dealt him, even as he could never forget its effects. Like the medieval alchemist, he had now transmuted dross metals into gold, failure into success, and become the maestro; the judge of equestrian skills, and his early life-changing sacrifice at the edge of the jump had later become the seal on his credentials. He had given his all in the learning of this craft.

Naturally, the Kingman family banking money meant he was never in any financial discomfort, no matter what his physical limitations were. I made a note to probe that aspect further through Cody's connections. Certainly that kind of money can protect a person from his mistakes. Isn't that what big money is for? The rest of us are condemned to own them and learn what we can from them; a fate I willingly embrace.

But when I looked at Max as a portrait subject, always my way of putting up a mirror to any individual, I did not see a man confined to a wheelchair. I saw something else going on, an authority not bound by his lack of mobility, but I would probably need a palette and a clutch of brushes in my hand to figure out what that was.

Max, of course, was already having his portrait done in a different medium by Amanda Klein. I don't think he needed me. I don't think he even knew who I was. Often that works in my favor.

CHAPTER EIGHT

Returning my empty glass to a server, I touched base with Maya, who was still happily working the crowd, and decided to take a look at the scene of the break in, the pantry storage room beyond the kitchen. With a glance over my shoulder, I went through the swinging door and found myself in a butler's pantry, full of cabinets and counters, trays, and wine glasses. Along one wall was the bar with a small copper sink the servers worked from. Dozens of wine bottles were ready to pour. Through another swinging door I entered the kitchen. Not much activity was happening inside, since the dinner preparations had been relocated to the tent near the barbecue.

Turned away from me, an old woman knelt on the floor in the far corner, fingering a rosary. Her white hair was cut short above her collar and her rotund figure strained against her white cook's jacket. Above her on the counter was a single plate of rice and beans next to a round woven tortilla holder. Puzzled, I didn't disturb her prayers any further as I walked over and opened the door opposite the dining room entrance. I caught my breath as I flipped on the lights.

In the center of the floor a man's body lay face down. It brought me instantly back to my own situation of four months earlier, when I was trapped on the burning roof of a hacienda with no way down. As often as I've seen it, I'm never prepared for a dead body. From the clothing I'd glimpsed earlier at the party, I knew it must be Raul Sanchez. Still hearing the subdued murmur of the woman's prayers in the background, I knelt down at his shoulder. His arms were both pinned under him as if he'd tried to push back against his own death. The telling detail was the crudely carved wooden handle of an ice pick protruding from the base of his skull, with only about an inch of the blade exposed. Within his dense hair, no blood was visible. He was not breathing and I could locate no pulse in his neck. I tried to think when I had last seen him in the party crowd. It had been about twenty-five minutes, possibly more, but other than scanning his interaction with Maya, which had mostly been confined to following her around, Raul had never been my primary focus, so I wasn't sure. When I noticed him last, he had been talking to a woman guest, but I couldn't recall now which one.

I had been less than fond of Raul, but there is no shortage of men who think themselves irresistible to women, and that's not usually a death sentence. Even so, I was not altogether surprised. If nothing else, here was a strong confirmation of Maya's low-grade uneasiness about Rancho Aria. Some people would be leaping to the conclusion that Raul had been killed by someone's husband, but I was not so hasty, since that seemed too obvious.

I knelt beside him and touched his neck. The body was still quite warm. It was only minutes since he'd been alive. Not a nice guy, probably a predator of women, but I still couldn't help but feel saddened by his death.

Even as I touched nothing beyond searching for vital signs, I saw no more physical evidence other than the ice pick, which, even with its rough handmade grip, still looked anonymous to me. Kitchens, particularly those with staff—and in this kind of upscale house, the kitchen would always have daily staff, and more for a party—are high traffic areas. Even with most of the cooking focused outside, anyone could have picked up that implement from a drawer or countertop and walked away with it in his sleeve, waiting for a moment to plant it in Raul's neck. There may have been several ice carving tools laying about where the horse head sculpture was done, and it would've been finished just before the party began to keep melting at a minimum. But how would anyone know Raul was coming this way? It made me wonder who he was most closely connected with among the staff. Had someone sent him to the storeroom on an errand, where he discovered his murderer waiting?

It might be no more than a moment or two before someone else came into the kitchen, so I rose and locked the door behind me. The door on the opposite wall led outside, and it stood open five or six inches. I stepped through it into a loading and service area, reached by a narrow lane through the trees wide enough for a single vehicle making deliveries. There would be parking for two more. In one corner was a utilitarian table with four plastic chairs. A single spiral light bulb hung from a cord directly above it on a line that came from the house. No one was there. The lock of the door had been pried loose and was still not repaired. I returned to contemplate the body of Raul Sanchez.

Aside from the male bartender and two male waiters, I had seen two young and attractive female servers picking up trash and empty glasses, taking orders to pass on to the waiters, and generally making themselves useful. The appearance and manner of both these women placed them as residents of the campo, but even so, had they also made themselves look available to Raul? A scene like this would be a way to meet some upscale friends, if not wealthy gringos, and connecting with a local man who had a firm and relatively well-paying position like Raul, might provide a huge advance in status.

The rust-colored floor tiles around the body told

me nothing. Collectively they were no more than the surface Raul Sanchez had fallen on, and in the process had left no message other than that this was the place where he was killed, because I couldn't see anyone trying to move the body unobtrusively through this crowd. It was ready for the crime scene tape and the body outline. After that, what could this tell us? I wanted the forensics van, and for that I knew I needed Cody, who had a finer eye for this kind of detail than I did. I had no idea where Maya was, but she could be easily lost as she worked a crowd, particularly at an equestrian event at this level.

Grasping a shoulder that felt, through his jacket, lifeless as a slab of meat, I pulled the body partially over and found by touch the outline of a wallet in the inner pocket. I didn't pull it out; that was for the police. I had no gloves and I didn't want my own prints on it. His cellphone was in his other jacket pocket. The motive was not robbery. I didn't care for the look on Raul's face as I drew out my own cell and took a couple of shots of the corpse before I turned it over and punched in the number of Diego Delgado of the Judicial Police.

After a rocky start on our first two cases, Licenciado Delgado, a prosecuting investigator, had become our mainstay contact within San Miguel's official criminal justice system. We were now, if not buddies, then at least comrades in crime solving, and we had learned to share information beyond the protocols on both sides that normally discouraged it.

After a moment he answered over the muted buzz and banter of a crowd. Was he here at the party already?

"Where are you?" I said. He knew my number well enough that I didn't have to identify myself, and in police emergencies you could skip the formulas for polite chatter that began any call.

"I am in Guadalajara for the annual police prosecutors' convention. I expect you have a crime to report. How awkward, since I am just now enjoying a shooter of Azul." This was a brand of tequila *reposado* that Maya and I had also recently discovered.

"*Salud!* I know you hate to hear this when the gringo community is involved, but there has been a murder during a barbecue party at the Rancho Aria."

"*Madre de Dios!* (Mother of God!) Not at Casa Kingman!"

"Exactly my thought."

"Who was the victim?"

"The trainer, Raul Sanchez."

Delgado especially disliked any murder of influential people, whether expatriates or not, where he often found that other influential people threw up obstacles in his path. We had experienced that problem two cases before, where the San Miguel police had been paralyzed and kept from investigating the death of a young girl from Veracruz. I could understand his reaction, but I wasn't ready to tell him that while the victim was not a gringo, the killer may have been. A moment of silence followed as I tried to recall whether any of our other cases involved an expat killing a Mexican. Nothing came to mind. In our experience at the Paul Zacher Agency, the expats here mainly prefer to kill each other.

"I am going to have to ask of you a big favor, Señor Zacher."

"*A sus ordenes, como siempre.* As always, at your service." This was a blatant exaggeration, but I had nothing to lose.

"Please take charge of the crime scene there and gather evidence. I hope Señor Cody is with you. I will not be back for three days, since I am presenting an important seminar in two days on gringo crime. Do you understand this?"

"*Sí!* Mostly." I thought I grasped the politics of it easily enough. "Crime with gringo victims or gringo perpetrators?"

"Victims, of course. I am almost certain it will be picked up by the U.S. media. And one more thing, if you will. When you have finished with your evidence gathering, please call Licenciado Según after you dial the regular police. In my absence he is covering my cases."

Licenciado Eduardo Según was an upcoming rival of his in the Judicial Police, a man of lesser experience and rank who coveted Delgado's job. We had seen them butt heads in the past. I signed off and called Cody. After asking who the victim was, he said he'd be on the road in two minutes. As far as I knew, no one had come into the storage room between Raul's death and my entrance, except probably the cook. I relocked the inside door as I left and put the key in my pocket. Anyone wanting to go in from the party would have to talk to me first, barring the presence of other keys. The outside door I was not able to lock because of its condition.

The cook stood up and looked at me uncertainly. The name embroidered on her smock was Ofelia.

"What did you see tonight, Ofelia?"

She shook her head, trembling. Clearly, her desire to avoid involvement was intense. Tears began to ooze out of her eyes.

"Again, what did you see? No harm will come to you."

"Only the body, *señor*. That is all. I saw no one with him."

"Did you tell Señor Kingman or Señora Montgomery what happened?"

She mutely shook her head again. I understood this. It was not her business to get involved in such matters. Being the bearer of bad news was beyond her job description. She might have been blamed for Raul's death, and most Mexicans prefer to avoid confrontation.

"I'll take care of it. Say nothing until the police arrive."

I walked back through the butler's pantry and returned to the party to wait for Cody with my earlier festive mood somewhat dampened.

Picking up another glass of wine at the bar and wandering through the group, I didn't pause to speak with anyone, merely observing people's behavior. Casual and relaxed was good, but too casual was not. I realized I had a sudden problem: the guard would not let the unfamiliar Cody through the gate. He'd only been there once before on the morning of the train derailment, and no casual visitors would be admitted during the party. I'd seen Carlos check us off on a list when we arrived.

Two minutes later I spotted Maya talking to a tall Texan wearing designer jeans, a leather vest over a pale blue shirt with mother-of-pearl buttons, and a black cowboy hat. I caught her eye.

After she excused herself I asked her to go to the front gate and persuade the guard to let Cody in.

"We have a problem?" Her expression froze and only her voice responded.

"Raul's dead in the storage room with an ice pick in the back of his neck."

"I'm on it." She left without another word, and although her face had registered a hint of shock as she turned, crisis never flustered her. I stood watching her move through the crowd for a moment. Nothing more would happen until Cody arrived, and I continued to study the gathering for revealing behavior.

As I turned, Phaedra Montgomery stopped me. If she had visited the kitchen recently, or more particularly the storeroom behind, she showed no sign of it.

"Are you truly enjoying yourself, Paul? You look so serious today. I was told by someone here that you have a wonderful sense of humor." She paused as if waiting for me to prove it.

I laughed at this idea. The moment seemed to call for it. "It's just that I'm so impressed by this wonderful property. You and Max have made an amazing home here. I especially love the art."

"Those paintings belonged to Max's great uncle. He was a close friend of Leyendecker when the family still lived back East."

I noticed that her makeup had been freshened. It was a version of what I had seen earlier, but denser, ratcheted up as if to better project over the footlights into the audience. I was no further away from her than before and it now looked more like a mask. Was she the first suspect?

"Well, I just want to give you permission to let yourself go a bit, all right? Whether you know it or not, you are kind of a celebrity in San Miguel. Not everyone can do what you do. Do you ever jump?"

"What a question!" I wasn't sure what she meant. Seeing Raul's body hadn't made me jump. "Only when I'm startled."

"I'm sure." Her look gave me nothing more to work with.

With Cody about to barge in with his forensics equipment and police attitude, and Phaedra's position as hostess, I debated whether this was the time to say anything about the passing of Raul Sanchez. I didn't want to provoke a rush into the storeroom, and I wanted Cody there in charge of gathering evidence while it was still untouched. To find myself concealing a murder was unusual, but shouldn't Max be the first to know? If that was the case, the conversation I'd never had with him was now coming in short order, and under conditions I could never have imagined.

"How is Max feeling tonight? It's a big crowd." I said, trying to mimic the tone of an insider, one who recognized the limitations of the old man's range of movement, even as he tried to be the most welcoming of hosts.

"Jubilant, of course. He's the center of attention, and the bloody expert on every equine question. Why do you ask?"

"Today I suddenly feel the most urgent need to talk with him, although he and I have never exchanged a single word before."

"Well, you go and do that, then. Shove all those young women off to the side with your elbows." She turned and walked away. "But carefully, they bruise quite easily, especially around the ego." This came after I had already moved several paces away myself.

I decided to sort her comments out later, after I had talked with the man, if I could find a way through his crowd of admirers.

Grinning and nodding at the few people I recognized, I walked through the crowd. Maya wasn't visible, possibly still down at the gate waiting for Cody. I found a group outside on the terrace under the lights, where the bartender serviced their needs off to one side. This was clearly not my crowd. Max hadn't moved; he was now the focus of six or seven young women looking down at him. As I came from the house, the only one I recognized, even from behind, was Diana Freeman.

It was the tight blond hair, smooth as satin cloth, knotted into a small immaculate bun, the black slacks that lovingly defined every muscle in her legs and butt, and then the Prussian blue silk top that illuminated her skin and hair. Her four-inch heels gave her two feet of elevation over the perpetually seated Max Kingman. The effect was tight but expressive.

Max's wavy hair was brushed back on the sides, and inflated into a fashionable contour on top, but the effect was that of a thin structure supported by oil or lacquer. In the right light you could have seen right through it.

Two of the women were Mexican, both in their mid-thirties, with the pale skin and perfect coiffures, exquisite shoes and flawless makeup of the upscale business class of the capital city. I knew without asking that they would've already looked this way at breakfast. They spoke to Max in Spanish and he answered in English. Had she been standing next to me, Maya would have summed both of them up in five words, because that was her own background. She had gone to school in Mexico City with women only about five years younger than they were.

"You will find that our boarding rates here, while not the cheapest, are aimed at attracting a certain quality of rider. We don't embrace beginners at Rancho Aria, either as our clients or their horses. Our trainer likes to begin by correcting the mistakes made by other facilities, and that can take awhile." Where did that old desert trail rider Drake Wilson fit in with this? With his simplistic and overconfident attitude, Maya had described him as an accident waiting to happen.

I wondered how exclusive Max could afford to be in the future, now that his trainer was lying dead in the storage room. Trying to listen for Cody's voice back toward the front of the house, I came around to face Max's wheelchair, which I began to see as a kind of podium from which he could address a group. The row of young listeners did not part for me and I spoke over the shoulder of one of the Mexican women.

"Is it the skill of the horse trainer here at Aria that makes the real difference?" I asked harmlessly, as if I had just walked in off the street to this party.

Without recognizing me, Max displayed an unruffled look, as nearly as he could from an eye level more than two feet below mine. At least he did not feel challenged by what I'd said. "Partly that, but also the quality of the supervision here. We overlook no detail in caring for horses and educating riders. Aria is the premiere equestrian facility in the upper half of México."

I knew enough from Maya to understand what he meant—that the best riders were in the north, especially in the western states up near the border where the *charro* tradition thrived.

"I don't think I've met you, young man."

The circle parted for me to move up and shake hands with him. "Paul Zacher. My partner boards her horse here, Maya Sanchez."

"Ah, Maya and Martina. They're both still off their former pace, of course, but coming back in tandem, I think. Maya could be good once again if she stays with it. And what do you do?"

"I'm a painter, and occasionally I investigate crimes."

"Of course." He nodded as his tone took on more familiarity. "I recognize the agency name now. I believe your people took out Luis Arteaga last year. No one else could've done that, certainly not that sap, Diego Delgado. How's the crime part of your business doing now?" Max Kingman accompanied this with a wry smile, as if he knew we'd had only one other case since then. Perhaps the detective business, like some others, was seasonal.

"I feel like it's picking up again, but nothing slows the painting."

"Arteaga must have been a tough one to bring down, though. His position was untouchable, by the police, anyway."

"Aren't they all untouchable to someone? But he had nothing on us, so he couldn't hold us back. Still, I've never met a killer that was easy to bring in."

During this brief exchange I had been studying Max's body language. Nothing moved below his waist, but the dynamic of his arms and hands did not appear to be trying to compensate for his lack of muscle tone elsewhere. I thought his breathing seemed normal, unlike that of some other paraplegics I had observed, but I also knew that this varied from person to person. His need must have been to come across as mostly normal. I felt I was out of my depth, as I had since we came in. The Agency had worked a number of cases where I'd felt handicapped, but never to the degree Max was. I recalled that Maya told me once she had come across a fictional detective character who was a quadriplegic. I wanted to move the conversation away from crime, although it was coming up as big as a headline as soon as Cody arrived.

Max had the finely lined skin of a smoker, but I saw no ashtray near him, and no one else in the group was smoking.

"I'm surprised at how well you're able to keep up with things down at the ring and the paddock."

He looked at me in surprise. "But that's my business. Don't you find yourself looking carefully at everything around you, even if you're not painting or investigating a case at that moment? You cannot stop recording the scene you're seeing even when you're off duty. Your fingers come up to frame an image, and your mind's eye mixes the colors."

That was all true, and more insightful than I expected from a non-painter, but I could also always walk up and take a closer look from ten inches away. If I had a portrait client, I could ask her to open her mouth so I could see what I wanted to paint about her teeth.

Max's ring of female admirers had not found any way into this conversation and, sensing an odd tension developing, they began to move inside, one by one, some with a small gesture of affection toward our host. I had sometimes heard Maya describe helpless or elderly men as cute, although this had never included me even at my most inept. With an edgy movement to his eyes as they tried to hold mine, Max watched them slip away. Soon the last one was gone and his expression lost its cheer. I hadn't moved. His striking blue eyes, matching those of his great uncle in the Leyendecker painting, riveted me.

"What is it now? I think you have something to tell me." Although a frown collected on his brow, his composure and mastery of the scene did not slip much in spite of a sudden awkward tremble in his hands. Surely this was the smallest part of his nerve damage, although I had detected no lack of nerve in his manner. Whatever he was missing, he was still in charge at Rancho Aria, and he knew it at every moment.

No one could hear us now, but even so I stepped forward to lean over his chair. "I just found Raul Sanchez lying dead in your pantry storage room. An ice pick was buried in the base of his skull. I thought you should be the first to know. I've already summoned my partner and the police. I know them and I'll handle the police when they get here, if you wish." I didn't want to say it was only Cody who was on his way at this point, since we were so irregular without Delgado's presence. I didn't know what to expect from Según, and Delgado had been clear about what he wanted from us.

After what he'd said about him, I also wondered how cooperative Max Kingman would be once Delgado returned to take over the case, but that was not our immediate worry. That would be between them, not that it was up to Max, now. I might already have upstaged him by calling Delgado before I spoke to him, but I consider myself an officer of the court, although I don't know whether that term is used here.

A moment of awkward silence followed my statement, during which Max's expression did not change much. If anything, a calmer look came over his face. "Raul was alone when this happened?"

This was not the reply I expected, and drawing back in surprise, I wasn't sure how much my face changed in response. But he wasn't looking at me. His expression was calculating as he stared down at the marble table, moving a single finger across it as if looking for a fine layer of dust.

"He must have been, aside from the killer. But what are you thinking? Were you expecting a *double* murder?"

Max shook his head without emphasis. "At least." His hands came together in fists and he pressed them against his chest.

I considered this for a second with the odd impression that he had been somehow prepared for this. Max's position in his bedroom or on the terrace beyond would've allowed him to see the detail of what went on in the paddock quite well, even if he couldn't hear it. My first impression was that what just ended in the storeroom had begun in the paddock.

At that moment I heard Cody's voice booming at the door, calling my name. Suddenly I thought of Maya and her inarticulate forebodings. I knew Max and I would have a lot more to talk about, but this was not the moment. I made a quick goodbye and rushed inside.

CHAPTER NINE

Maya had met Cody at the gate and I'm sure she filled him in as they walked up to the house.

He was plowing through the crowd in my direction, three inches taller and forty pounds heavier than anyone else. From the half-defined bulges around his waist when he approached the terrace I knew he had all the requisite equipment: his gun—a .38 police revolver that could not jam, a pair of cuffs, a box of twelve extra cartridges, a spray can of mace, and an attitude that said, "Don't mess with me if you want to walk away from this." Without understanding why, the crowd parted willingly before his urgency. He was vibrating.

I converged on both of them and waved them toward the kitchen. Ofelia was nowhere in view as we passed through the two pairs of swinging doors. Maya stayed at the dining room door to intercept any other traffic as I unlocked the storeroom and flipped on the light.

Cody dropped to his knees and bent over the body. I said nothing as he flexed the victim's fingers, scanned the fingernails, and turned the head enough to touch the eyelids.

"About an hour, more or less, I'd say. You must have come across him not long after he died. Anyone see anything?"

"Maybe the cook, Ofelia, but she was incoherent when I came upon this."

He leaned closer to the ice pick handle without touching it. Drawing on his latex gloves, his fingers minutely raked the hair surrounding the entrance wound. This went on for some time before they stopped.

"Here it is," he said. "This fatal entry is the second attempt."

"What do you mean?"

He waved me over and I dropped to the floor next to him. His separated thumb and forefinger flattened the trainer's hair to reveal a fresh circular red puncture mark on the skin the diameter of a wooden matchstick. It was about three-quarters of an inch higher than the ice pick. If any blood had seeped from that tiny wound, it was minuscule.

"Here's the first try. The pick must've hit a vertebra, is my guess, and hardly gone in at all, less than half an inch, stopped by the bone. Then it was pulled out and thrust back in, where it entered between two vertebrae the second time and fatally pierced the spinal cord."

"And you think that first miss tells a story."

"Always."

"Sure, if you can read it. I don't know if I can. Did you ever have the nurse fail to locate a vein when she's drawing blood? And she's a professional. She does it twenty times a day." I could hear Maya in conversation with someone at the kitchen door but I didn't turn around since the tone sounded benign. That probably wouldn't last much longer.

"Maybe it tells us more about what the killer isn't. The angle of penetration is also an issue. You met him, what was the victim's height?"

Here is where the exact visual memory of a painter comes in. It's not always operating, but it came back again at the right time. "Five ten and a half, I think." A good height for a Mexican man, but nearly two inches shorter than I am. "Isn't the real question what reaction Raul had when he felt the pick go into his neck the first time? Didn't he duck forward trying to get away? Did he shout?"

As the trainer lay face down with his head angled to the right, the handle of the ice pick emerged at a slightly upward angle, indicating a downward stroke from behind. But I couldn't read the detail beyond that. The tiny initial wound changed the game because it must have launched Raul in a downward motion of escape, pulling away from the blow. The forensics people could try to take the angle from that one. We weren't equipped to do it.

"As always, we'll need a little backstory here."

"I have some, but not much."

After Cody scanned the storeroom floor and shelving, and searched Raul's pockets, I called the regular police at 066, just as any gringo would do who didn't know that murders are handled by the Judicial Police. Then I called Licenciado Según. He said he was leaving immediately. The sound of his voice suggested a wolfish glee in taking a case away from Delgado.

Aside from a keychain and a few coins in the front pants pockets, the wallet contained the usual items: a driver's license, a membership card to a Guadalajara equestrian organization I didn't recognize, 320 pesos in bills, two condoms, and three business cards from women that Cody stuck in his own shirt pocket. "Max Kingman may still be out on the terrace," I said as I locked the storeroom door again behind us.

"He's the ranch owner?"

"Yes, and he's at the core of the ambiguity Maya's been talking about."

"You're saying I should interview her after I talk to him?"

"Definitely, and better you than me, but now I think it's your turn to interview Max out there on the terrace. I sense he has some psychological issues that fall within your area of expertise, not that there's much that doesn't. I'll wait here for the police."

No one remained in the kitchen as we left the storeroom. Ofelia may have gone outside from the terrace. In the great room the crowd was nervously milling about, sensing something was amiss, but I wasn't sure that any of the guests had left. I said nothing to anyone, waiting for the police to arrive and furnish the proper authority for whatever they did next in situations like this. If they were like us, it was never the same twice.

CHAPTER TEN
CODY WILLIAMS

Cody peered through the open French doors for a moment before emerging onto the covered terrace. Seated at a circular table a man in a wheelchair faced away from him toward the darkened hills to the east. Beyond him at the edge near the garden a broad-shouldered man with short legs sat silently on a bench, his muscular arms folded, waiting as if Cody's appearance was expected. Smoke curled away over the barbecue, and in the tent next to it three men in white coats and chef's hats worked at a long table.

As usual, Cody took nothing for granted as he stepped onto the tiled floor, closing the door softly behind him. His notebook waited in his back pocket, but he wasn't ready to bring it out.

"Laszlo, bring the man a real chair, would you? Get rid of these plastic things. Don't know why she's always trying to save a dime." Max Kingman didn't turn toward him. His voice was low and steady, and carried little of a specifically Texas accent.

The man called Laszlo leaped up, cleared away three white deck chairs, and placed an ornate cast aluminum armchair facing Max. As Cody came around the table and sat down he noted with satisfaction that he would be able to watch the inside action over Max's shoulder as they talked.

"Max Kingman. I'm the owner of this spread." His right arm gestured toward the darkened hills behind the house. He rolled out into plain view as Cody leaned over to shake his hand. Max was wearing a pressed pale blue western-cut shirt, with mother-of-pearl buttons on the pocket flaps, and newish jeans with a clear, ironed crease down the front of each leg. He was not wearing boots, but loafers with a mellow mahogany shine. They showed little wear. Without mobility, a single polish would probably last him a year, Cody thought.

"You must be one of the Paul Zacher Agency people," Max said.

"I'm Cody Williams, just an investigator for the Agency team." His thirty years as a homicide detective in Peoria was not something he wanted to bring up yet in this context. Perhaps not at all. Demonstrating a lower status and using an informal tone would be the key to making this interview a success. He heard Laszlo moving about behind him, but Cody didn't turn. He had studied the man in detail near the entry gate on the morning of the wreck, and again as he approached the table coming in.

Although more than a little eccentric, Laszlo appeared to be just what someone would prefer, Cody thought, as an assistant to a disabled older man. His almost simian arms may have been what people noticed about him first. They ended in wide sturdy hands, backed by a grizzle of black fur. His head was angular and too large. With his square jaw, in the right light it almost had corners on it. His thick black hair grew down to his ears and was parted in the center. Without anything overtly hostile in his manner or gestures, he still conveyed a sullenness that might have been no more than a certain set to his protruding jaw.

Laszlo's movements were brisk and efficient, and he somehow seemed beetle-browed and ominous at the same time. He rarely spoke, and when he did the soft character of his voice and his Hungarian accent made him difficult to understand. If he didn't shave twice a day, he should have, just to soften the overall shadowy effect. If in some ways he resembled an animal, it was not a party animal. Paul would've wanted to do his portrait; Cody thought the painter could get some interesting effects with that unusual cranium in the proper angular light.

At the same time he wondered why Max wasn't able to wheel himself around, by his own, as they would say in México. His arms appeared to be undamaged, his shoulders robust, his grip firm when Cody shook his hand before sitting down. Nothing about Max above the waist was feeble. The ranch house, large as it was, presented no challenge to a wheelchair, since it featured all the principal rooms on the main floor. The doors were oversize in width. As he passed through, Cody estimated the openings at about forty-two inches. Max could shoot through them without slowing down.

Cody had observed that many handicapped people take pride in the mobility they're able to generate for themselves. Independence is a value worth maintaining to the degree they can achieve it, and they prefer to avoid the appearance of helplessness that's suggested by having an attendant constantly on hand. He wondered why Max was underlining the point that he needed help, or was it only to show that he could afford it? Having money added a more complex dimension to any suspect.

Walking up from the gate, Maya had told him that Laszlo was in the background nearly all the time, as if he never went off duty. Raul had mentioned to her his constant presence and how hard it was to get a conversation alone with Max. Cody realized that when he looked over at the man, he tended to do so covertly, although he wasn't sure why. Was there something less than trustworthy about him? If Laszlo was really Max's bodyguard, who would wish to do the older man any harm? The white lab coat Laszlo wore was loose enough to conceal a gun. Cody also wondered whether he might have some hold over Max. Was it psychological? Financial?

"You and Mrs. Kingman have had, as Paul Zacher told you, a murder here tonight. The regular police will be coming shortly, and then the Judicial Police, but before they arrive, I need to find out what you can tell me about it."

"It's Montgomery. Phaedra kept her own name. What is your official capacity in this?"

"This investigation will ultimately be handled by Licenciado Diego Delgado of the Judicial Police, but he's away on business for the next few days. He asked Paul to have the Zacher Agency take a look at the scene, before Licenciado Según takes over. We've been asked to stand in for him before." This was an exaggeration, although they had often shared their case notes.

"I've met Delgado on another matter. He's the kind that would need some outside help." Kingman offered no further comment.

"I understand that Raul Sanchez was your trainer. That's a key job in any equestrian facility."

"Indeed. He kept the lower orders functioning here. Trainer goes both ways, as you know."

If Cody caught an ambiguous note from this, his face gave nothing away. "So the term 'lower orders' would cover both the horses and the riders?"

"In a few cases, but mostly the riders, where I cannot always be as selective if I need to cover expenses and make a dollar or two, which we usually try to do here. We take more pride in our horses, since we have more control there. You buy them or not, and when they are foaled here, we can assess their conformation and their potential. If they're off the mark, they're sold on the strength of their bloodlines. The main thing is that the better animals can do things their human riders often find beyond their ability. We also always try to pair up the potential between horse and rider if you don't board your own animal here."

Nodding, Cody pulled out his notebook. "I'd like to take a few notes, if you don't mind. Just to get people's names and ages right. Addresses and occupations, that sort of thing."

"No problem." A sly inward look followed as he reached toward the table and lifted a wineglass to his lips. Before he set it down again, Laszlo was there to refill it.

In the overhead light from a wrought-iron chandelier hanging from the canvas brace on a short chain, Cody thought Max's broad face was marked by an imbalance between the inflow of alcohol and the outflow of sincerity. He would be telling anyone from the Agency as little as he thought he could get away with. That was nothing new. Cody's practiced instincts were picking up a hint of something not quite right about Max Kingman, although this early, he could not have said what that was.

He smiled broadly, showing better teeth than Max had. "I still am a cop, I guess, just less formally than before. I enjoy the work. Always did, even when I got shot at."

"Well, then I can tell you that I am a connoisseur of all things equestrian, so now we'll understand each other better. If you saw me in court, it would be on the stand as your most expert witness. No one has ever shot at me, although I'm always careful going around corners." Max smiled too, for the first time. Perhaps, as his face suggested, the opening cards were now all on the table, and the rank of connoisseur was far higher than that of cop, even if they might be close on an alphabetized list. "Laszlo over there is also my bodyguard."

Cody made a few marks in his small notebook. He tried to never do them at the same time as he received the information they recorded.

"I'm surprised that you need one, considering the security at the gate. Has anyone at the ranch ever tried to do you any harm?"

"Not physically. But I can see them thinking about it sometimes."

"Is anyone here tonight in that category?"

"No. They would not have been invited." He brushed this idea away with a broad stroke. "I'm a good reader of people."

Cody filed this statement away to bring it out at a better time. "Would you say you are a well-liked person, Mr. Kingman?"

Max smiled ironically. "No one as good as I am at what he does can avoid provoking some envy. So, no, I wouldn't say so, except by my staff, of course. I am their *patrón*, as you can readily understand. Whether I command the *respect* of everyone boarding here is quite another matter from being popular, and the one that's most important to me. Why do you ask? I wasn't the victim tonight."

"But in a way, you were. Some people insure their key employees. Did you have a policy on Raul's life?"

"No, but now I wish I had. Silly not to have thought of that, but he was a young man, no more than forty."

"How would you assess Raul's performance here at the ranch? As a good reader of people, I'm sure you've thought about this in some detail."

"With the horses?"

At this implicit option, Cody paused, unable to read Max's look beyond the raised eyebrows. Maya had given him no background on Raul as they walked to the house and he was coming at this with little background.

"But wasn't that his job, Mister Kingman? The horses, I mean?"

"That was certainly what I hired him for five

years ago."

"But then another element crept into it?" As Cody knew, some people tended to rewrite their job descriptions without aid from management. Perhaps Raul was taking advantage of Max's immobility to acquire greater control over daily operations.

"You could say that."

"But what do *you* say?" Cody wagged his pen before him.

"Only that Raul himself was at stud here. Privately, I thought of him as Mádrigal II, but without the stud fee income."

Cody paused for a moment to think about how to approach this. Max's frankness might have simply been his manner, or he may have been spinning this description for Cody's benefit, trying to suggest a false motive for the trainer's murder.

"My associate, Paul Zacher, told me earlier that you had a stallion of the same bloodlines as Mádrigal, one that was still a major disappointment at stud. I believe his name was Countertenor. Apparently some of the more powerful qualities do not breed through in every case."

Max Kingman gave Cody a level look. "We call it breeding *true*. Yet, at this rancho, we are all musical, playing our own tunes. You might say in that context that Raul was a baritone at the top of his form. I never heard a single note of falsetto from the man as he pursued the sopranos across the turf. I'm sure that's why he's now lying dead in the storeroom among the cans of pickled jalapeños and sacks of dry frijoles. But finding out why he came to this end, that's *your* job, isn't it? So how did our man die? Paul Zacher said he was killed with an ice pick."

"Yes, an ice pick in the back of his neck. It punctured his spinal cord."

Max Kingman whistled softly. "How ironic. There was not a single chip of ice in that man's body. If I were you I would start by looking for a killer with an exquisite sense of irony."

"I am starting to appreciate yours. Might you be a suspect in this?" Cody's steady gaze did not waver as he leaned forward. He was suddenly conscious of how much greater range of movement he had, compared to the crippled ranch owner.

Max looked him in the eye. "Are you suggesting that Raul was fucking Phaedra? Because no one else's activities here are any concern of mine in that respect." He waited a long moment for a response, but Cody could outlast anyone in an interrogation. "Anyway, look at me. My physical limitations are obvious. Had I made a beeline for the storeroom to murder Raul, the path I plowed through this gathering would've caused a stir that many would recall. On the other hand, there are two steps up to the threshold on the outside door to that room. While I do have one copy of the key, to me they're insurmountable. I would've had to bring Laszlo in with me as a murder witness just to get up those steps. Maybe you should talk to him after we finish here."

"I was suggesting nothing. I only ask questions in these situations, and I have to ask them all, even when they're not comfortable to answer."

"As for Phaedra," here Max laid his hands palm downward on the table and leaned forward, "my wife is a woman of immense dignity, and from a very upper class background in England. I have seen her family's former country home in Sussex, and their origins go all the way back to the family of Catherine Howard, the fifth wife of Henry VIII. The estate was unfortunately lost to inheritance taxes in the fifties and Phaedra was born in their London townhouse. The years following the War were such a crisis period for those old families. When she was working in the theater, her roles in London's West End were those of society women in every case, once her abilities emerged and she became established."

Cody let these remarks hang in the air unanswered for a while. "Can I ask how old you are, Mr. Kingman?"

"I turned sixty-eight three weeks ago." His look suggested he had accepted this burden with no joy, and it was far from his first disappointment.

"And how old is your wife?"

"Fifty-one."

"And you have been married for how long?"

"Fourteen years. Naturally, she retired from the stage at that point, welcoming a return to the kind of country life she had mainly known through her friends in England, even if it was here, so far from her roots."

Cody pretended to record this with a flourish.

"Had she been married before that?"

"Never, never, although she had many suitors, of course." Max grinned fondly at the thought. "I understand that Alan Bates wanted to marry her not long after her stage debut. Her real break came with a small part in *Noises Off* in '82. Bates is dead now, of course."

When Cody tried to do the math, he guessed that Alan Bates might've been nearly thirty years her senior. He decided not to pursue it. "And you?"

A look of discomfort crossed Max Kingman's features. "Oh, I was married at the end of college when I was twenty-two. Of course, my family frowned on that relationship. She was on the staff at our ranch outside of Austin. It was a grand place. Most of that furniture you saw in the great room, and the art, of course, came from that house."

"Was she a Mexican woman?" Cody was guessing. He hadn't so much as glanced at the furnishings as he rushed through. Usually he was more observant, but he wanted to examine the crime scene before it was disturbed by partygoers.

"Yes. She was just a girl, really, but very beautiful. I believed I was in love."

"Believed?" Cody sometimes felt his voice was too deep, even too harsh, to express more delicate sentiments. This was one of those times.

"Maybe it was only that. Who can say now? But I was too young." Max gazed out into the hills, his expression unreadable, although his disability did not prevent a shrug. "Back then, you know, I very much resembled my great uncle Alistair. Perhaps you noticed him in the paintings in the great room. He's the one with the horse. It was Alistair who started our equestrian tradition and I was given his name for my middle name. He had the lean focused look of a hawk. Everyone said I looked just like him."

So eager was he to see the crime scene, Cody had noticed none of these paintings coming in. The party could've been held in a tent, nor did he see anything hawk-like in Max's face. His jowls sagged onto his collar and his eyelids drooped. A fine network of ruptured capillaries laced his cheeks. Moisture dotted the corners of his mouth. Max took another sip from his glass, rolling the wine under his tongue for a moment. It occurred to Cody that he was probably drinking a much better vintage than what was being served to the guests.

"Excuse me for just a second." With a subtle gesture in the direction of Laszlo, the attendant leaped to his feet and ran over to him. Cody moved away from the table for a moment while they spoke in a low tone.

From the edge of the terrace he waited with his arms folded and made a point of observing Max's communication with the man. It was mostly low-key, as if they had been together for a long enough time to know each other so well that a single gesture spoke volumes to him. Laszlo's face was mobile and his responses were often based on a lift or tilt of his heavy eyebrows. In addition to speaking, Max used an occasional hand signal, fingers mostly, delivered from close to his abdomen. He could've used these to direct Laszlo where to move him without interfering with his other conversations. In a moment the attendant moved off toward the barbecue and the kitchen tent.

Cody sat down at the table again as Max wheeled himself back to his place under his own power. "How long did that first marriage last?"

"Until about a year after my injury. I was paralyzed from the waist down in a fall, and I was twenty-four when we split up. I don't think I'll ever forget how she looked, but it was no longer right, you know? She didn't get much from my family, although she tried. As it happened, my grandfather owned the district judge who heard the divorce case. That's how it often was there.

Still is, I'm sure. In any case, I made a decent provision for her myself. My family was happy since they didn't care to have it carved in stone. Is this background check really necessary? I find it tedious. Much of this you could find on the Internet."

"You can't ever know how necessary it is, but it's no more than routine in a case like this, Mr. Kingman. I always prefer to hear it first hand. That way I can watch people's delivery."

This did not cause Max to blink. "I'm sure it would only be relevant if you thought I killed Raul. I can assure you that I did not. His death is very damaging both to me personally and to Rancho Aria as a business. I know you must always consider that old detective rule of who benefits from the crime. That in itself should tell you I could have had nothing to do with it."

"Still, you don't seem very distressed."

"I'm definitely distressed, I'm just not surprised."

"Then who do you think might have killed him? Let's look at that benefit aspect again." Cody was not about to take advice from suspects. He eased back into his chair and set the notebook on the table, pushing it to one side, as if the less formal part of the interview had begun. It was now time for opinion more than fact. Hearsay and speculation were admissible.

"I think you should look at the women who board here, or their husbands or partners. In that circle, you will have your work cut out for you."

"Anyone in particular?" Cody's pen was suddenly poised in the air, as if he had concealed it in his palm all along, but he didn't bring the notebook any closer.

Kingman waved any specifics aside. "Any and all. Maybe they pooled their boutique coffee money and hired a hit man, I don't know. I've heard you can take out a contract on someone for a thousand pesos over in Los Rodriguez. A gringo victim may cost you ten percent more."

On that day's exchange rate this came to about $62.00 U.S. Eleven drinks at a boutique coffee bar, Cody reflected. Los Rodriguez, a rough and ready farming community in need of occasional supplementary income in the dry season, lay just a dozen kilometers beyond those trackless darkened hills behind Rancho Aria. Just far enough away to have not heard the impact of the stone-laden truck that caused the train derailment. The possibility of a roving migrant being the killer had never left Cody's mind after Paul's call that afternoon. Maybe one had returned for a second helping of groceries when Raul happened to walk in. Maybe one was a prison escapee fleeing a life sentence for murder. You could never tell. He made a mental note to examine the door to the storage room again.

"I've heard that about a contract too, and it's come up before in the Zacher Agency. But let's move on." Cody didn't give the hit man idea much credence. "I thought I saw Renée Bontemps when I walked through the crowd inside. Do you know her well? Because the Zacher Agency encountered her as a witness in an earlier case." Cody was privately wondering why Paul hadn't mentioned that she rode at Rancho Aria, although the phone call from Paul that brought him out to look at the murder was mostly confined to basic facts. Perhaps he was planning to get to it.

"Look at my eyes!" Both of Max's palms went up, as did his eyebrows. "Do you think I'm blind as well as paralyzed? It is my greatest frustration that I see women like Renée boarding here, and then Laszlo wheels me away to bathe me or help me do my sorry exercises. Or take my medications." He craned his head toward the bulky silent man now back on the bench, who did not move in response. This wasn't one of his cues.

"What kind of meds are you taking? Pain?"

"No, there's no *physical* pain anymore. Antidepressants, anxiety, insomnia."

Cody gestured broadly. "This is not the spread of a person with financial problems. What do you have to worry about now?"

"Something like this, what happened tonight. In a small city like San Miguel, now we have a situation that damages my reputation, scares off my clientele, and disrupts my concentration."

"Does that suggest you saw it coming?"

"Only the tension is what I saw building up to this, just reading it with no facts. So if I don't seem surprised, it doesn't mean I anticipated that Raul would be murdered. Don't you ever get a feeling about something before it happens? Don't you ever pick up a playing card off the table and know what it is before you turn it over? Tell me the truth."

Cody waited for a moment before going on, reminded of his girlfriend, Sheila, who had that ability to occasionally visualize both future and past events she could never have known about. She was unable to summon this skill on demand, so her value to the Paul Zacher Agency ranged from occasionally profound to usually zero.

"That doesn't happen for me." This was not quite true. Cody now and then saw a person ahead on the street that he would never expect to run into. But when he approached, he found he was wrong, it was only someone with a vague resemblance to the person he thought he had seen. Then ten minutes later, he would actually see that person. This was the only kind of event that ever happened to him that he thought was at all paranormal, and he rarely dwelled on it.

"So now you've had forty-five years in this chair," he continued, trying to regain the thread, "or a series of chairs like it. Your leg muscles are atrophied and you have long ago accepted life as you have it. What does that mean today in terms of bitterness? Because given that background, you have still decided to place yourself in an atmosphere of championship horses, beautiful women, virile men, and pricy properties. You could have retired to the beach in Puerto Peñasco and drunk rum as you watched the sunset slide beneath the waves every evening. For a lot of people, that's what México means. For many gringos, that's the *real* México."

Max merely looked back, shaking his head, as if Cody would never get this.

"None of this makes you look that good personally in comparison with your surroundings, so what is the process I'm looking at here tonight? Many important people have come out for this party, and possibly, as the murderer must see it, they're all going to be suspects in this killing. This suggests premeditation. Is there an element of control in being in this position that you cannot get any other way? I'm going to suggest to you that, whatever your harmless aims with this party, if you did not kill Raul, or have him killed, someone else has taken that control from your hands. Perhaps that was the point. Maybe I should be looking for someone who wanted to destroy your credibility."

"Ha!" The shout ripped from Max's throat, without waiting for Cody to finish. There was more derision than humor in this exclamation. "As if, investigator that you are, you could ever imagine how pathetic my life is already. I wake up every day reminded of what I don't have. The beginning is always less than zero when Laszlo lifts me out of bed. My daily goal is to claw my way back to what I was yesterday, but that's not all."

"OK. What else?"

"How old are you, Cody?"

"Coming up on sixty-three next month."

"So you know what I'm saying."

Scraping on the tiles, Cody pulled his chair a bit closer, since Max's voice had dropped as if they were entering a more confidential terrain. Yet, only Laszlo was still with them on the terrace, and he was too far away to hear. A subdued buzz came from within the house, and from the other direction, a cool breeze washed down from the darkened hills. The cook tent staff was packing up the unused dishes and silverware.

"I'm not sure I do know. I mainly know that I'm no longer young, but I have never for one moment thought I was finished. My girlfriend is nineteen years younger than me." Cody hadn't intended to bring up this personal element, but he refused to accept the invitation to identify with Max's disability just because they were close in age. Cody had been shot four times over the course of his career and he was still standing. His private motto, one he had never revealed to Paul or Maya, was *No excuses*.

"I can see y'all are walkin' around, but are you still that sharp as a detective? Tell me the truth now. It's only between two old guys."

This was a question Cody asked himself at least monthly, if not daily. "We'll see, won't we, in this case? I plan to prove it to you, and I'm sure we'll talk again, Max." He rose with a nod and went back inside, folding his notebook into his back pocket, thinking he had left still barely in control, just enough to open the door to the next conversation with Max Kingman.

When he passed through the French doors, the crowd was still restless and unfocused inside the great room. It seemed thinner now. He wasn't sure how much he had gotten from Max, but he knew more would be coming. Looking through the group, he recognized Drake Wilson, Amanda Klein, and several local Mexican ranch owners that he knew only by sight and in other contexts. In a far corner stood Renée Bontemps with a glass of white wine in her hand. Paul was moving toward him with a look of having something to tell him.

In a sudden rush the local police stormed through the front door as if a civil disturbance were in progress. Guns were drawn by cops in armored vests. With a handshake Cody and Paul greeted the captain they already knew and stepped back while all the other guests were gathered in one end of the great room for an initial screening. As Cody yielded control to the police, Paul looked around for Maya. He found her coming out of the bedroom complex at the left. Next to the entrance of that corridor was a second powder room. Paul's face was a question mark as she edged past the crowd toward him. Her expression was unreadable.

"Where were you?" he whispered. "The cops are here."

Maya gave him an investigator's triumphant face. "In Max's closet. Where else? Clothes make the man, am I right?"

Not only was Maya the determined master of English idiom and slang, but Paul knew that wardrobe was one area where women's eyes often saw better than his. "And?"

Moving closer, she looked around to be sure no one else could hear this. "Paul, Max Kingman's shoes are all worn on the bottoms. Some even have soil in the little spaces on the soles. Every pair!"

"Every pair?"

"Well, all of the five I looked at. He had about ten more, but I didn't want to hang around. Why would you need so many shoes if you can't walk? He must not only move around inside the house, but outside too. How many others know this? Certainly Phaedra, and also that gnome of an attendant of his."

"Laszlo."

"The grounds crew too, unless he only goes out at

night."

Paul's eyes met Cody's over her shoulder. Nodding, he was pulling out his notebook, and Paul's first thought was that he needed to talk with both Cody and Amanda Klein again, and soon.

CHAPTER ELEVEN

When two paramedics walked in with a stretcher the cop on duty at the door waved them toward the kitchen. No one was in a hurry. I stepped forward and gave them the key to the storeroom. Word of the crime had by then passed through all the guests and nobody was talking about anything else. A moment later Licenciado Según entered with two of his staff and spoke to the officer in charge. We lingered at the fringes.

I had expected Según to be larger and more imposing, and to have more hair than he did, and that what there was of it would not be creeping back in front with the rest trimmed very short. I had also thought his eyes would be bigger and more intelligent. Perhaps he would also have more of a roll around his waist, being mostly in a desk job, but he didn't. Surely he would've been dressed no better than his superior, Delgado, who usually wore a series of third-rate brown suits in differing shades, but I was wrong again there as well.

I went over and introduced myself, saying I was the one who'd found the body and called him. After a few questions about the time I'd discovered it and whether we had disturbed it at all, he took my name, address, and phone number and said he'd be back to me after he processed the crowd. Según recalled that we had met before on another case—I hadn't been sure he'd remember—and he didn't seem to regard me as a suspect.

A few minutes later I left Maya talking to Cody and caught up with Amanda Klein as she was released from the great room staring at a black ink stamp on the back of her hand, as if she had paid admission and could get back in if she wished. Passing a confused server who still had a tray in his hands, she picked up a full glass. I gripped her elbow and guided her out to the rear terrace. She didn't seem surprised. When we were through the door I pointedly pulled out a chair at an empty table and got her seated where no one would now be fed. When I finally spoke, my voice sounded like a hiss, but after what had happened that evening, I didn't care.

"I think you forgot to tell me something important, Amanda. Max Kingman can still walk!"

She shrugged elaborately and drew off about a third of the wine in a gulp. "If I revealed that kind of thing to everyone who just came up to me on a porch, no one would buy my book."

"I'm not everyone, dammit!"

"Besides, it took me three months to figure that out. You're a better detective than I am to get it this fast."

"I hope so," I said. "Maya looked in his shoe closet while everyone was being rounded up in the great room by the police."

"I thought of it but I never got a chance to see the bottoms of his shoes. He doesn't like people staring at him or taking his picture. He said it makes him self-conscious." She held up her empty wine glass to me as if a refill was the price of more revelations. Her coy grin suggested she wasn't stressed, but I knew she was.

I walked over to the bar at the edge of the terrace and got her glass refilled, picking up another full one for myself. The glasses weren't big enough to last through a serious conversation. As the crowd filtered in one at a time, most of them headed for the bar too. Through the French doors I saw more guests emerging from the great room after the police talked to them briefly and recorded their names and what they'd seen. None of these uniformed cops was qualified to do much more than that, and I knew we could get the list of suspects, meaning everyone at the party, from Delgado later once he took over from Según. On no other case had we ever had the official kind of leverage that his absence gave us on this one. I knew that as reliable witnesses to the party scene, Delgado would be eager to bring us in on his side so he could depend less on the prickly Según.

Max and Laszlo had disappeared.

"You're not going to put that in the book," I said. Amanda was still thinking about Max's mobility.

"Of course not. I work for Max, and he doesn't know that I know. Besides, I think I referred to our bond of trust earlier."

"Doesn't seem to go both ways, does it? And how did you find out?"

"Once I got up during one of our conversations to go to the powder room, and out of the corner of my eye I saw him lift one leg and scratch beneath it. He didn't use his hands to lift it. Naturally, I didn't let on that I had seen him do it."

"How do you think that looks now, in this context?"

"I don't think anyone knows that except you and me, and Phaedra and Laszlo, of course. They would both have to be in on it."

"This is a murder case now, Amanda. The Zacher Agency has been asked to act as a surrogate for one of the judicial police investigators until he gets back in a couple of days. Do you think Max might have killed Raul?"

"Why? Just because he could've? What would his motive be? I don't see it."

I studied her for a moment, wondering whether she was interviewing me. For the party she had tucked her pale blue shirt into a pair of dressy jeans, added a black string tie, and put on a suede vest over it. "Do you know anything about Raul?"

She pulled out a cigarette from the pack in her shirt pocket and lit it. "Anyone who spends any time around here knows about him. Raul Sanchez was a world-class sportfucker. That was his game. He would screw anything that moved. Although he was a great horse trainer, too, this job was even more an opportunity to connect with the local talent in a classy setting. Every woman who has walked onto this property wearing riding boots and tight breeches knows that. In this classic tragedy of which we're seeing the first act tonight, think of it as *Carmen on the Pony Trail*, his role was the doomed Latin Lover." She gave me a sassy grin.

"Sounds like he was a busy man."

"You can take the measure of that yourself. Just ask your own cute Mexican girlfriend. I'm sure Raul has had his hands all over her, although frankly, he usually prefers American women. Maybe to him it was all a payback for the loss of Texas and California, I wouldn't know. Most likely he needed no more reason than chasing his dick, and the blondes here tended to give it a special heads up. Excuse me for smoking, but this is getting a little more twisted than I like. I prefer a more gradual buildup to a climax than we're getting here."

"Tell me you're trying to quit."

"Aren't we all trying to quit something? My

goal is to quit giving interviews before this damn book is published."

"I can see that."

"But I always have to smoke at parties, especially when there's a murder before the food is even served. Maybe the kitchen will pack it up to go for us."

We fell silent as two couples came out of the French doors and walked toward the bar murmuring something I couldn't catch. I didn't recognize them and they didn't look our way. The women both wore short, tight skirts with black cowboy hats and boots.

Although I could barely keep myself from snorting at the way Amanda expressed her analysis of Raul, I also had to appreciate her candor. On top of Max's unexpected frankness, this was building into an image of the late trainer as a guy with a target on his back that increased in size with every conquest he made. I thought again of Max's remark about the Los Rodriguez sixty-two dollar contract. What an easy way out! One thing I've learned in the detective business is that México can be a dangerous place, but mainly if you happen to get a little too dangerous yourself to other people. Otherwise it's always been a walk in the park for Maya and me.

"Would you be able to make me a list of Raul's conquests?" I had little hope she would, but I had to ask. There were times when she didn't mind sharing, but more often, not.

Amanda shook her head as she blew smoke into the soft evening breeze. "Would Raul himself have been able to? Would he remember them all? But no, I only know that I'm not one of them. The rest of it is definitely not my problem. I never ghostwrite kiss and tell type memoirs."

"But I heard you used to write bodice rippers. That was another thing you quit."

"That's true. At least the research was interesting."

"Anything else you can give me, like would Phaedra be on that list? She might've been out of his normal age range, but what guy like him could resist doing the queen bee? She'd be the biggest notch on his bedpost."

Amanda took the last sip from her glass. "Look, I'm not going to play that game where you say a name and I nod or shake my head, OK?"

"Like is it bigger than a breadbox? I guess this is not *Twenty Questions*." Who even knows what a breadbox is anymore?

"No, it's not."

"Let's go back to Max, then." My voice dropped in volume. "When you discovered he could still walk, what did that add to your picture of him, regardless of whether you thought you could use it in the book or not? Wouldn't information like that, particularly of that magnitude, flesh out the picture for you in an important way?"

Amanda turned around and checked that no one was close enough to hear us. "You want the bottom line answer?"

"Always."

She pushed her empty glass toward me as if I was having an attention deficit problem. I was back with both refills in less than a minute. Fortunately the bartender was still not pouring a big serving.

"I've thought about it a lot and I believe Max had a major failure of nerve after that fall so many years ago."

"OK. Go on." I wished Cody could hear this, but he was tied up elsewhere.

"I do know that he'd already owned five different horses by that point, starting from when he first rode in competition at fourteen, and that part will be in the book. He told me with apparent candor that it was always because they didn't work out for one reason or another—it was never any shortcoming of his. Riding had been important in the Kingman family for three generations, since his great uncle Alistair, and when he wasn't making progress, his parents would buy him another horse. He was never allowed to falter in his development. They bailed him out in high school too, by smoothing over a couple of disciplinary problems he told me about. Maybe more than twice. I knew he once stabbed a kid in the thigh with a scalpel in biology class."

"The family was always walking along behind him, picking up his garbage," I said.

"That part was a narrative separate from the fall, but I put them together in my own mind because I thought they were connected. He doesn't always tell me everything, but my sense is that he has never had to face the consequences of anything in his life that didn't go just as he expected, or worse, not as his parents felt it should."

"So, not ever having to own his mistakes, he didn't learn anything from them, which would've been the normal process we all go through."

She thought for a moment before she replied. "That's what I've been getting from his story. The unspoken subtext was that he would've seen how his mom and dad were always running interference for him, and he easily might've come to expect it, because that had always been his history. He never got hurt, no matter what he did. And of course, in acting that way the parents would've been good, well meaning people, I'm sure."

"Privileged is the word that comes to my mind. Pillars of the community. And the family fixed his divorce, too."

Amanda crushed out her cigarette. "Of course, but while their banking money went a long way to keep things like that at bay, they still couldn't have saved him from that fall at the jump. I'm surprised Max even went for it."

"Because he didn't have to take any chances like that?" I asked.

She took a long pull at her wine and, with a touch of drama, stared up into the night sky, which in this case was the coarse yellow canvas of the canopy six feet above our heads. It must have been disappointing to someone looking for a longer perspective. "My idea is that his failure of nerve happened not before, as Raul suggested to me, but immediately *after* that jump, like that same day, even within the hour. Maybe before that moment, he didn't realize yet that his parents couldn't fix everything; it had always been so automatic that he never had to analyze his choices. Then, lying on the ground and hurting, he couldn't face the possibility of their desertion."

"Not that it truthfully was that."

"Right, but it must have seemed that way to him. It was a new kind of reality, one he'd never been allowed to experience. His response was that he chose to be too damaged to go on."

"He was twenty-three then," I said, "so he covered it up. He wouldn't ever need to try again because he was confined to that wheelchair. That was a drastic kind of risk management."

"Yes! He constructed a new kind of reality for himself. And the injury was the horse's fault... You're probably thinking this is too far fetched, too twisted. What's your take on this bit of backstory? I guess you know something about people." She took another long sip from her wineglass. Her hand returned to her left front pocket under the vest, but shrank back from the cigarette package and came up empty.

"Because I paint them?"

"Exactly. I've seen a couple of your portraits. To me, they were painted from *inside* the subject's head. That can't be an accident. Frankly, I think you and I are in the same business. I don't mean detective, although that's not a stretch for you either, is it? I think you see things differently."

Amanda was not making me any more comfortable, and I was surprised how pointed her analysis was. "What would his parents have thought about this sudden self-induced roadblock to Max's jumping career? They would've been talking to his doctor too." I was trying to move her along from the focus on what I did.

"Maybe they went along with it to protect him as usual. Of course they're both dead now."

I slowly shook my head. "It's one of my core beliefs that people are capable of believing absolutely anything. I mean that literally—anything, although this is an extreme example. If Max has lived that rationalization for forty-five years, then his entire life has been informed by a lie."

As someone devoted to a painting career that gives my own life meaning, I had wondered in the past how people settled for anything short of that. Maya believed that many people lead self-deluded lives, making excuses just to get by every day. She had come up with this from her history research, constantly trying to understand people's motives.

Amanda shook her head. "But Paul, is that so rare? A lot of people live with their spouses in relationships without love, all the while talking themselves into keeping it going. Maybe it's for the sake of the kids, or because their combined assets are too small to divide in two parts and have both get by. Sometimes it's merely to keep up appearances. Or as so often here, their religion doesn't allow divorce so they offer their misery up to God, hoping for a higher place in heaven because they booked some of the suffering in advance. Maybe they can skip purgatory that way."

"I don't think you can say it's delusional, though, in Max's case, if you saw him move his leg under its own power when he had to scratch it. He knew what he did that day, because he must do it all the time. He just forgot you were there, or thought you were beyond seeing it and the itch was driving him crazy. You're a household regular now, and he feels he can act differently around regulars. It's an ongoing fraud, and as you suggested before, Phaedra and Laszlo have to be in on it too.

They won't ever say anything because they're fully vested in it."

"No, they won't ever say anything," she said. "Why would they trash their legend? What would they gain? If they were to expose him they would also reveal their own complicity for all these years."

"Tell me more about Phaedra Montgomery." Now we had developed some real momentum.

Three more guests emerged as Amanda gave me a quizzical grin and fell silent, leaning back in her chair until they had gotten their drinks and settled at a table closer to the barbecue than to us.

"She's a veiled one. I've had a total of one brief interview with her."

"And?"

"She gave me the perspective on Max Kingman that would come from any person living with a crippled spouse. It sounded *generic*, as if she had researched it online before she talked to me. That was all. She offered nothing about herself. At the end I felt I should be grateful for the ten minutes she spent with me. It was a one-act play called *The Disabled Spouse's Patient Wife*."

"And at that time you didn't know about Max still walking."

"No, because that was early on, like at the end of the first week. I was looking for background from her, a way to form some questions to him that would be revealing in ways I hadn't thought of. So you can see how valuable Phaedra has been to my book."

"Are you going to try to talk to her again?"

"No. She didn't spend her early years in the theater for nothing. I think it's your place now to take her on, not mine. Imagine that you're painting her portrait in some ways."

"I have." But I didn't think I should be the one to do the next conversation.

Here I was reminded of a stylish movie from the mid-fifties, starring Cary Grant and Grace Kelly, *To Catch a Thief*. The title reference belongs to an earlier axiom: *It takes a thief to catch a thief*. In this case, the thief would be Maya, a stealer of truth from the unwary, our own head of the Paul Zacher Agency, who should interview Phaedra Montgomery Kingman. More than Cody or me, Maya could avoid putting Phaedra on the defensive, and she would know better than we could what she was looking at, in her hair, make up, clothes, and manner. I had not forgotten how well she'd handled Ruth Bendickson, a best-selling author, in the case we filed as *The Book Doctor* not so long ago.

I hadn't seen Maya for a while, and since Amanda was already looking for her next glass of wine, I excused myself and went back into the great room. Maya and Cody were probably conducting some subtle interviews of the boarders who had come out of the first level of interrogation. As I passed through the French doors I spotted them across the great room standing near the entry with Licenciado Según and three armed policemen. I held off for a moment, thinking they were probably saying goodbye. For the Agency to connect with Según on good terms would be an astute public relations move until Delgado returned. We weren't going to have a chance at any serious private conversations with this kind of assembly line questioning going on in an agitated crowd.

I waved at them unnoticed. Their conversation appeared to be heating up. Maya gestured toward the kitchen, and then downward with both hands in a gesture I read as, No way! Without any warning as I watched, two of the cops seized her arms and cuffed them behind her. Always ready to defend her without thinking, Cody whirled and lashed out with a powerful left-handed uppercut and dropped one of the uniformed cops to the floor, where he didn't move again. Según seized a pistol from his belt and leveled it at Cody's head from inches away. The other cop pressed his gun to Cody's back.

Had we changed sides in an instant? I was paralyzed. As much as I wanted to butt in, I had no gun; in fact I had lost it in the fire on our last case, and guns were suddenly the only currency with any value. The cops hustled Maya and Cody through the door, and I followed as far as the front steps to see them moving in heavy security up the slope to the parking corral. As they disappeared near the cars, I pulled out my phone and dialed Diego Delgado again, muttering to myself until he picked up.

CHAPTER TWELVE

Although I had spent some time privately with Licenciado Según early on that evening to describe my discovery of the body, the only positive outcome I brought with me when I left Rancho Aria later was the early promise from him that they would email me the party photos as soon as they downloaded them from the camera. He clearly thought that was a liberal concession, and in some ways it was certainly more than he had to do. On the other hand it hardly compensated for arresting two-thirds of the Paul Zacher Agency at such an early phase of a case we didn't know we had. But with them in jail, we certainly had one now. At least they were still in a holding cell, and not in with the general population. When I called downtown later to find out what had led to the arrest of Cody and Maya, he declined to say, only asking me to call him tomorrow. I tried not to think he was going to invent some phony charge and needed time to research it.

My final query was whether I could see Maya

tomorrow, and he shut that down immediately. He felt he was already being too generous by sending me the photos from the party. Any question of visiting either of them would have to wait until he had finished interrogating them. He did not want to risk, he said, any contamination of their stories by outside information. I realized that I would've been much more upset if Delgado hadn't been coming back in less than three days.

Back home on Quebrada later that night I sat in the half-lit great room facing the computer with a stiff cognac and a bad attitude while I downloaded the six files containing the photos from the Rancho Aria emails. As background, I put on some Navajo flute music from Carlos Nakai. It seemed to smooth out my brain waves, which felt as kinky as steel wool. Over the fireplace, my seated portrait of Maya as Frida Kahlo stared across the room at me from a less stressful time. I had changed out of my party clothes and put on a pair of ripped paint-spattered jeans and my dark blue tee shirt that said STAFF on the back, my comfort outfit.

Scanning the group, I pulled out the four shots where Raul Sanchez appeared. One caught him at the edge of the frame. Naturally, as an employee, albeit an important one, he wouldn't have been featured in any of these photos, which had the feel of a promotion for a magazine spread, or someone's equine society column. Here the trainer was facing a woman who was partly turned away from the viewer, but from her figure and clothing it was clearly Diana Freeman. Her back had that subtly distinctive arch at the base of her spine I had noticed before. Raul's face held an expression of anger, even indignation in response to whatever she was saying, but it offered no hint of the pain from his back injury. He must have been medicated. Would that numbing have masked the first ice pick blow to his neck? A more telling detail was that Diana had seized his wrist with her right hand, and from the nuance of the muscles and the indentation of his skin, it was not a gentle or friendly grip.

She must have been looking for something from him, literally trying to pull it out of him. The modest bulge in the inside muscle of her forearm expressed a determination that drew him toward her, but it didn't tell me any more about what her relationship was with Raul. Maya had told me earlier that from what she observed in the paddock, Diana ran hot and cold. Sometimes she flirted with the trainer, and at others she barely noticed him when she was not having a lesson.

"In passing by, her chin goes up," she said, "and Diana looks away, beyond his shoulder."

"How does Raul react to that?"

"It tortures him. He can't tolerate indifference. He would rather have you hate him than not care about him at all. I think he's used to being hated. It's closer to love than indifference is."

An uncomfortable thought. Although I had done no more than look at her for an instant when she said this, now that she was locked up, I wished I had explored that idea further. Particularly, I wanted to ask her if she had ever heard he was abusive with women.

I leaned back in the chair for a while, trying to picture Maya at that moment. I saw myself showing up on the other side of the bars with a glass of her favorite cognac and her blue flannel comfort nightgown. Her own toothbrush and the toothpaste she favored.

In another shot Raul stood talking to Kyle Winokur, a man I knew slightly as a retired dentist, although he was only around fifty. I didn't know he was a rider and I hadn't noticed him at the party earlier. His manner was graceful, with refined features, and his presentation read slightly effeminate. Drake Wilson, the safe trail rider, stood next to him, but looking elsewhere, not connecting. Thinking of the ice pick in the upper spine, I felt that Winokur would know something about anatomy from his dental school studies, perhaps enough to locate the space between two vertebrae on the first attempt, or would it still take two? In the heat of the moment, it might.

In the third shot, Raul was looking over his shoulder at Renée Bontemps. She was just entering the frame with one arm extended, and her expression was not visible, but his look was familiar in a way I didn't care for.

Perhaps it was only hopefulness I saw in his face, and not quite the naked leer I might've called it had I not been in my objective investigator's mode.

At the party I had seen her again later on, but only briefly in the company of a much older and elegant Mexican man, one who had to be from the capital, because they display a certain privileged look. He was wearing a white western-cut suit with ten-thousand-peso boots that might have been custom made in León, our nearby leather industry capital. My impression was that I couldn't have afforded his haircut, much less any of the clothes he was wearing. Money would always gravitate toward Renée. Much of it would bounce off.

This man wasn't looking at her then, the kind of indifference that would force her to work a little. I'd never been able to summon that much effort from her, since Renée had usually encompassed my entire attention in any conversation in our last case, and there was never a single moment when she didn't realize it.

I studied all the photos in detail for about an hour more, but I was far from fresh and much less than objective, a little tipsy, and more than a little irritated at the way things had gone. I backed up the file, shut down the computer with a careless gesture, and went up to bed. Glancing in the mirror as I brushed my teeth, I didn't see much to impress me, even though I was the last man standing at the Paul Zacher Agency. Even that much success seemed mostly accidental.

During that night, through the screened open windows on both the Quebrada and the garden sides of our second floor bedroom, the dense unmistakable scent of skunk assaulted my nose. Perhaps I was dreaming and the skunk was only a metaphor for the latest foul turn of our investigation, but it smelled real enough, and the air in the bedroom was thick with it. I turned on my elbow to see the clock. It read half past one. I'd only been in bed for an hour.

While I remember them from Ohio, with the peculiar waddling walk they favor, I have never seen a skunk in México. Maya always tells me I must have smelled a *tlacuache*, a variety of possum, as we would call it in the north. But here the *tlachuache* is a sinister, ugly customer frozen in your midnight headlamps, caught scampering in alarm across the road as you return from a party, as if interrupted in some dodgy business they couldn't risk in daylight. A blotchy black and white, they look dirty in a most repulsive way. Being filthy is one thing, but when it also stinks it's far worse. With a body two feet in length, beady black eyes, and a long rat's tail an inch in diameter; you hope you don't meet him later in your dreams, but perhaps I had.

I reached out to draw Maya against me as I rolled over trying to forget this. She could generally make me forget almost anything, except her presence. It was only when I realized why she wasn't there that I fully awakened, wondering how angry she must be locked up in a cell on the Doctor Mora Road.

Unable to stop thinking about horses, I didn't fall asleep again for a long time. Gradually I was beginning to see the equestrian world as an amplified metaphor for the normal world we lived in, with all its features written in block capitals. Its emphasis was a matter of scale, inflated by money or ego, or simply by the effort and expense of maintaining an establishment like Rancho Aria. Still, on the surface, and as physical as it was, it moved with a calculated grace and a measured rhythm. I was surprised to find myself clinging to the edges of this equestrian company, because I had never before needed to take up that much space. Although some have large properties here, most homeowners in San Miguel live on lots of three hundred square meters or less, from which they carve a small patio or garden.

But horses require real acreage. You need to have their friends over, whether for just hanging out for the night, or for serious breeding, which is somewhat like an important prom, one where the corsage is more likely to be eaten than worn. Sudden romance between two 1200-pound animals that lack the backseat of a car to frame it was not something I wanted to contemplate in any detail, even though I had once owned a well-used

Buick station wagon from the sixties. Yet, it was always that too-specific detail of breeding that crept into my mind when I was off guard.

Two *hectáreas*, for example, would be about five acres north of the border, and that much land would work for your horse and his or her friends, as well as his normal everyday companion. Because when their friends leave, horses do not suddenly become tranquil loners, eager to contemplate a broad unpopulated landscape. They are herd animals that need at least a burro or a pony for company, a friend to turn around and greet once the gate has closed behind the guests. Otherwise, feeling like they've taken a wrong fork in the trail that could be full of ugly surprises, they're not happy, and you don't want to have an unhappy animal seven or eight times larger than you wandering over your property. Because of my erratic schedule with the Agency, and my need to avoid distraction when I'm painting, I had never even wanted a dog, and the commitment that Maya had now embraced was far greater than the largest of dogs.

Martina, for example, has a monthly board bill of around $500. This is about what Maya and I spend on food for ourselves, even though we don't eat hay, but there are two of us, and we eat well, while Martina is a vegetarian, shunning premium smoked turkey breast and fajitas, and marinated *arrachera* from the barbecue. Fortunately, Martina knows nothing about organic produce, except for the carrots Maya buys for her at the Saturday market. What would organic hay cost? Or is all hay organic? Some nuances of this are still beyond me.

For Martina this monthly fee also includes shoeing and routine vet care, while in comparison, Maya buys locally made Flexi shoes for herself, and neither of us needs worming that often. Our romantic encounters are more private, and if the earth occasionally moves after nine years together, the ground does not actually shake and shudder beneath us, so parallels with our new family member can never be that precise.

If we hadn't boarded at Rancho Aria, we would now need our own *ranchito* to support the activities of our 1200-pound pet. Horses need exercise, just as we do. They need longeing. This is a process of limbering up, where your horse runs in a circle at the end of an extended rope you hold while you utter hopeful commands, for example, *Don't pay any attention to that puddle! You've seen that rock a thousand times before! Keep your head down!*

Some riders longe a horse without the rope, using hand gestures, or pointing with a longe whip, but this is still accompanied by hopeful commands. However, hopeful commands are never part of the detective's technique, since they don't stand a ghost of a chance of working outside the round pen. For example, *give me your gun! Please.*

And then there's the issue of disposing of or

composting all that manure, thirty to fifty pounds a day. And what about the flies? Max's answer to fly disposal was too baldly prominent, too nakedly vengeful for my taste. Apparently he needed to hear them fry, one by one. Was he the *warden* at Rancho Aria, running his own private death row?

Finally, at an hour I failed to notice, I fell back to sleep and dreamed of hoof prints in the sand. At first it was a beach, but then, Maya cantered up Quebrada (in the wrong direction) on a tall, elegant jet-black Frisian stallion, full of restless spirit, with her hair loose behind and running on the wind. She was on her way home.

I awaited her on the front step with carrots in my hand.

CHAPTER THIRTEEN

On the following afternoon Licenciado Eduardo Según suggested we speak in English to help keep his skills active. That way he could better relate to the many gringo criminals he encountered. He went on to tell me he had lived in Los Angeles for eight years in his childhood, an experience he was grateful for, but had no wish to repeat. I didn't ask whether he'd been legal at the time.

His desk stood in a corner of the large second floor room where Delgado sat at a bigger desk in the center, under the fan that rarely worked, and even now had only two of its normal four blades. I assumed he was still at the convention in Guadalajara, and nothing else was going to get Maya and Cody released if I couldn't manage it during this meeting.

The advice Delgado had given me the night before was to stay calm and play along until he returned, as if I could do anything else. My visit to Según might help, and even if that didn't get Maya and Cody released, it might still give me a better idea of what the police were holding for evidence. Delgado also didn't fail to point out how the pressure was now fully on me to find the killer myself. His tone suggested he regarded this option with glee.

Coming in, Eduardo Según's posture was relaxed, and as I waited in a chair at the side of his desk, I watched him remove his suit jacket as if it had cost a great deal of money, which was a sorry joke. I'd seen better ones on the used clothing racks at the Tuesday Market for six dollars. He rolled up his shirtsleeves with precision before he began with a conventional and meaningless greeting, and then looked down at his notes as if he'd never seen that information before. He cleared his throat. I felt like this was an exercise in theater.

"I notice that you have been acquainted with Señorita Sanchez for some time, I believe?"

"Yes. We've lived together for nine years." My strategy was to deny nothing, if possible, and avoid arguments, as if full disclosure was my natural, even my preferred way of doing business.

Según's thin lips gave me a tight smile that suggested he was hoping we could both end up on the same side, but I suspected this dream would be fading quickly, as was my hope of persuading him to release Cody and Maya.

"I see. Sometimes we do not know people as well

as we think. In my career with the police, I have observed this too often."

His nod prompted me to nod in agreement, but I didn't.

"Maya Sanchez is a kind, intelligent, and loving woman. She comes from a business class family in Mexico City. (It never hurts to throw this in.) Her father is an important executive at Pemex. By education, she is a historian with an advanced degree."

Nodding as if all this were merely the typical smokescreen of half the killers he arrested, Según shuffled some papers and pulled out two from a file on top, spreading them apart to align them side-by-side. He covered his mouth with one hand for a moment, reading silently.

"So you are calling her Maya, yet I see here that this is not her real name." He removed his narrow glasses and peered more closely at the page.

"Yes, her real name is Maria Sanchez." I was certain he already knew this, since she'd been booked coming in.

He paused and looked at me soberly. "She is hiding from something by using a name not her own, I think? Perhaps she was a criminal in the past, even before you knew her?"

"No, it's a nickname, just as you would call someone Chucho, who was named Jesús, or Pepe for

José." His shrug followed, suggesting this was merely the first round—so far a shaky draw.

"There is also the question of the Sanchez family name." His pencil neatly circled it.

"What do you mean?"

"One possibility is that of a blood feud between Señorita Sanchez and the victim, Raul Sanchez. How closely were they related? Sometimes, as you can imagine, as with an inheritance, for example, conflicts can become brutal among family members."

"They were not related at all. Surely you know how common that name is."

"Possibly." He slid one of the papers around and moved it in front of me. "Do you read any Spanish?"

"All of it."

"What do you see here?"

Knowing what it had to be, I scanned it only to gain time. "It says that a few years ago Maya killed an American here in San Miguel by a blow to the head with a clay pot or sculpture. He was a prominent expatriate, forty-seven years old at the time of his death."

"And you are telling me that you already knew this?" He was nodding as if to get me to admit such a thing.

It was my turn to shrug. "I was there when it happened. She saved my life and the lives of two other people by killing him. Your sheet here does not say she was charged with any crime as a result." I placed my index finger squarely in the middle of it.

"Perhaps not, but I always look to the trend, do you see?"

So do I, and it wasn't going that well. When I offered no further response, he pushed the second sheet toward me. Then, as if reconsidering, he pulled it back. His finger traced along several lines. "Two years later, in the city of Guanajuato, just here I can quote it, '... and during this confrontation she pulled out a .32 caliber automatic pistol and shot to death the American woman named Mercy Buchanan. The bullet entered from the right side under the arm and passed through the lung and heart. The victim was naked at this time.'"

He leaned back and stared at me with his lips pursed, as if resting his case. "Once again, I must only guess that this naked woman was about to kill you, Señor Zacher. Perhaps you were naked too, although that does not appear in this report. I might be asking myself now why you are so unpopular that you always need a bodyguard."

I stifled a sigh. His approach was not that different from painting. You could look at an object and shade it one way or the other. You could make it look like something it wasn't now and never had been. "It may sound odd, but this report is true. And, once again, I really was present when it happened, and fully dressed."

"And you are not worried now?"

"About this charge with Raul Sanchez?"

"No, about the fact that she could turn against you any time. Señorita Sanchez is clearly a woman of small patience."

By this time I was coming up a bit short on that virtue myself. "I'm sure you will also see from your papers that she was not charged with any crime in that shooting either."

He drew his hands apart. "So perhaps the law enforcement in Guanajuato is negligent. I suspect that the investigator in charge enjoyed her looks and decided to release her. Who can say? Whether charged with those other murders or not, she has a violent temper, that much cannot be disputed. My concern now is that I don't know anyone else in San Miguel who killed two people and was still walking around free before we caught them. It is a good thing that we have her now."

I struggled to keep from laughing; I could've named several they'd missed, but I chose restraint over confrontation. "Of course, I can understand your concern. You have the tourist traffic to consider."

But Según was not finished tying this conversation into small, overly tight knots. This is why all these investigators in the Policía Judicial have a law degree.

"Is it also possible that Licenciado Delgado is a friend of yours? I have heard him speak favorably of you in the past. He says that when he is at your house he is always served the Herredura Añejo tequila in an elegant shooter, and despite being yourself a gringo, you are often very polite to him, although not always. I am wondering if this case will benefit from having a more impartial investigator now that he is off on the party circuit making speeches, as if he was some…"

"That Herradura is only a simple courtesy. He has never given us a pass on anything. If you were to come to our home for a visit, I'm sure you would receive the same."

The truth was that I'd rush to double bolt the door before that would ever happen.

"Indeed. Now I will tell you something that is not public knowledge. Our inspection of the victim's body reveals he was beaten earlier. The ice pick was only the blow that finished him."

"I saw no marks on his face when I discovered the body."

"No, but had you lifted his shirt you would have seen the two strong impact bruises on his back, one above the left shoulder blade, and the other further down, just above his hip. They were made by the same weapon."

"What was it?"

"We do not know this yet."

"What do you think happened?"

"We believe that your Señorita Sanchez had

a disagreement with the victim earlier and struck him several times with this unknown weapon as he tried to flee her anger. Later, thinking that the crowd at the party would offer many candidates to be the killer, she finished him with an ice pick. This, may I remind you, was an injury also delivered from behind, just as the blows on his back. It seems to be her usual way of doing business."

"This is all coincidence. You have no evidence to support it."

Según shrugged elaborately. "So you are saying now that she was on good terms with Señor Raul Sanchez? They were perhaps both active in the Rotary together?"

The character of their relationship was a question I'd been hoping to avoid. "She thought he was a good trainer and that he knew his business. That's all. I'm sure she had never seen him outside the rancho."

"I see. And all the horses liked him, too, I am sure. The Rancho Aria was nothing but a party of good vibes. You see; I know this term too. But how did it go personally between them?"

"I don't know. You would have to ask her, if you haven't already. It is only during the last three or four months that she's been boarding at Rancho Aria, and I've only visited a few times. Let me ask you a question. Did you find her fingerprints on the ice pick?"

"No. We found no fingerprints on that wooden

handle, since it was so crudely carved and the surface too rough. So that proves nothing either way. What did you think we would find?"

"Then the evidence is inconclusive."

"Not entirely." His eyebrows lifted modestly as he puffed out his cheeks. "We have a witness."

"To the murder?" Why were we having this conversation, then, if he knew Maya didn't do it?

"Well, not exactly. But there is a witness to the fight between Señorita Sanchez and the victim earlier in the day he was killed. This is for the time when he was injured."

Why hadn't Maya said anything to me? Was that why she was so upset before the party? I thought she had seen the evening as a way of reorienting her mood, not finishing someone off who'd insulted her. She doesn't hold a grudge; she has a short fuse, but once the fireworks are over, there are usually no aftershocks.

"Who would that witness be?"

Eduardo Según slowly shook his head, looking at me as if I were an apprentice in this business, a way I too often feel myself. "Of course, here in México we have a long history of witness intimidation, so you will realize that I cannot tell you the name of this or any other witness in this case."

"How about Cody Williams' position?"

"That one is easy. He is in jail at my discretion. If

Maria Sanchez confesses, we will let him go. ”

Now it was my turn to shake my head. “He would take a bullet for her.”

“I will keep that in mind.”

With a minimal farewell I walked away from Licenciado Según’s desk and downstairs onto the street facing the *jardín* with empty hands and the opening beats of a grand drumroll of a headache.

CHAPTER FOURTEEN

Back home I took three aspirin and threw some cold water over my face, but it wasn't ten minutes before the entry bell rang. Unlocking the door I found nearly the last person on my front step I would've expected, Drake Wilson. He was wearing well-worn jeans and a waist-length denim jacket, and on his face was an ingratiating but tentative grin. His right hand gripped a small black plastic garbage bag tied at the top. Still stewing about Según, I felt no great interest in talking to him, but there was always the chance that his visit had some bearing on the case.

"I brought you something." He raised the bag to eye level.

"I got enough garbage from the police already today. Come on in." As I closed the door behind him, he stopped halfway through the *zaguán*.

"Wow, you own *two* Diego Riveras?"

"No, I painted those. You'll notice they don't have his signature on the front. If you turned them over you'd see mine on the back." As we went out to the log-gia, Drake peered into the great room to check out the furniture and paintings but I didn't offer a tour, nor did I feel like suggesting we have a drink. He sat down at the edge of the garden in the wicker chair I usually sit in myself, which didn't gain him any points.

"I came to tell you a little story. My two daughters are in town from Albuquerque and we went out to the ranch for a trail ride this morning."

"Of course. I hope you didn't find another body." I was sure he had told them of the murder, a sample of dangerous México gossip to take home. As he spoke I glimpsed Orlando, our garden grackle, with his yellow eye glaring at us narrowly from the edge of the fountain. He doesn't take well to strangers on his turf.

"You know that passage in the fence where a fork in the trail crosses into the housing development, Las Campanas?"

"Right. I noticed it when I went out to look at the train wreck." Maya had told me earlier that the Rancho Aria property had once been part of a much larger parcel where premium housing estates had been constructed. When that area was sold off, the Kingman family had retained the right to run trail rides through the open spaces. At about 500 acres, part of its charm was that most of Las Campanas was left in its wild state, with different trails for people on bikes, on foot, or horseback.

A few of the residents boarded horses at Rancho Aria.

"When I stopped there with my daughters to open the gate, a man came out of the brush along the fence carrying this. He was tall, dressed in worn olive-colored pants too short for his legs. His hair was long and ragged. He was missing two teeth on the bottom, and his skin was very dark."

"Now you've got my attention. He must have been one of our migrants from the Devil Train. I figured some of them were still out there."

Wilson grinned. "He wanted to sell me what was in this bag for 500 pesos, a lot of money to him." When Drake picked it up and set it on his lap, I noticed how big his hands were.

"And so you bought it for about thirty-one dollars."

"Yep, I bought it. When I saw what it was, I didn't quibble." Nodding, he appeared to be playing some kind of game, one whose rules I didn't know. He reached into the bag and pulled out Maya's new show bridle, still wrapped in the clear plastic bag it came in.

"That cost 3,000 pesos," I said.

"I know. The price sticker is still on it and I figured it was easily worth 500 this morning. I saw Maya with it in the tack room when she brought it in last week."

I pulled out my wallet, but Wilson's hand went up.

"Hey, you don't owe me anything. That was only

my contribution to some desperate people. I would've helped them out even without this."

I thought I heard a twinge of desperation in his voice, unrelated to his charity. "I wish Maya were here to thank you for that, Drake."

"Next time I see her will do." A slight pause followed. "How much trouble is she in?"

"I'll get her out. Según's boss is coming back the day after tomorrow. Can I offer you a beer? I've got some Negra Modelo."

"That'd be great."

Wilson was seated facing our old carved limestone fountain with his hands on his knees. I watched him through the kitchen windows as I stood at the sink and poured the two beers into mugs, wondering if he was there partly to find out what I knew. Although his hairline was still robust in front, a circular thinning space was developing on the top of his head toward the back.

I came out and set the beers down between us next to a bowl of peanuts. My headache had fled.

"Awfully nice of you to do that," I said.

He only nodded. "I don't think you got to meet my girlfriend last night. Her name is Pilar Ruiz."

"I noticed her with you, but I didn't have a chance to talk to her. She's an attractive woman."

"Yes, she is that." He nodded, but the look on his face was troubled.

I waited, wondering if more was coming. "I always think it's interesting when I see American men with Mexican women. It's not that common; people often stare at Maya and me. Sometimes they accuse me of going native."

He nodded again, slowly. "Pilar used to live with Raul when I first started boarding at Aria."

He looked at me to gauge my reaction. To draw him out, I gave him nothing in response.

"You're not surprised at that, Paul?"

"No. I wouldn't be surprised that any woman used to be with Raul. What would surprise me is if any of them had stayed with him very long."

"She was sick of him by then and ready to move on. I could see that immediately, even if she didn't say it just in that way. It didn't take much to bring her over to my side of the corral." He smiled as if recalling the event as he took a long pull at his Negra Modelo.

"I suppose she got tired of his philandering. Any woman would."

"That, of course, because it went on all the time. Worst of all was who he was also sleeping with then, toward the end. I don't know, maybe it was at the beginning as well."

I picked up one of the shelled peanuts and tossed it overhand toward the fountain. I didn't have to think very hard about who Drake might be talking about. With a practiced move, both feet landing flat on the rough stone pathway as he came down, Orlando caught it on one bounce. "Bingo," I said. "Did Max know about it?"

"Max knows a lot. I assume he knew that too. No one really tells him much, none of the boarders anyway, because he's so critical, but he still knows what goes on."

"Did Raul talk to Pilar about his connection to Phaedra? Maybe you don't know. Maybe she didn't tell you that."

"He was arrogant enough to talk to her about his other affairs. That was part of what pissed her off so much. He constantly disrespected her by assuming she would put up with anything just to stay with him."

"Anything?"

"Well, just about."

"That doesn't surprise me either. Did Phaedra ever talk to Raul about Max's disability?" Without knowing what, if anything, that Drake knew about it, I couldn't be more specific.

"Not that he told Pilar."

"When was all this happening?"

"About a year and a half ago. As far as I know, it might still be going on with Phaedra."

Now I saw a different angle to this. If Phaedra had told Raul that Max could really walk, that might be a motive for Max to murder him. How could you trust the trainer with any information that dangerous? Max's lifelong lie could be cracked open like an egg. Since Raul was on a power trip, there was a strong possibility of blackmail. If Max had found a way to slip away from the terrace during the party, he might have come around and entered the storage room from the outside at the service area in back. I had noticed a wheelchair ramp next to the bar on the side closer to the service wing, but it still didn't seem likely. Laszlo would've seen him go, or even wheeled him over. I suddenly realized I hadn't thought that Raul sleeping with Phaedra was reason enough for Max to kill him. It's never helpful to make unconscious assumptions like that, but hadn't Renée suggested at the party that Phaedra was in some way key to this? Of course at that point Raul was still alive, so what she could have thought Phaedra was the key to might mean nothing now.

"This is what you really wanted to tell me, isn't it?" I almost whispered. We could have heard the leaves on my nearby lime tree rustle, had there been any breeze. But they were unmoving, as if waiting, as I was.

Drake didn't look at me. "I guess it was. After Raul was killed last night, I was trying to find an excuse to see you today without being too obvious, and when this bridle turned up, well, that made it so easy."

"And is there more to this story?" From his manner, I already knew there was.

Drake nodded but didn't speak. His left hand lifted in a helpless gesture and fell back on his knee. The other hand gripped his beer mug as if it were the only thing he had left. His gaze was fixed somewhere among the shadowy bromeliads. Their complex forms offered many interactions to contemplate instead of thinking about something else you didn't want to confront. He started to nod slowly. Somewhere in his thoughts he had come to earth.

"It's that I found out she was screwing Raul again, you know? Pilar. I couldn't believe it. About two weeks ago I noticed a bruise on her shoulder. She told me she had stumbled over my riding boots in our closet and bumped against the doorframe. But I have a rack for them and I never leave them on the floor before I put them up. You don't want to pull them on and find a scorpion inside. That asshole! I could kill him! I can't understand it. We were together more than a year and a half."

"So he had hit her?"

Drake could only nod again. "And I do know what that is. I saw it once before, years ago before I was married, a woman who wanted me to slap her hard when we were in bed. I did some research on it because it really put me off. It's that some women like a man that treats them like dirt, even treats them with violence. But I don't know why. I had hoped Pilar wasn't like that. I always treated her well. Now she's gone. She moved out this morning and she's staying with her sister."

"Do you think Raul's death precipitated a crisis in her mind?"

"It really looked like it. She started weeping in the car on the way back from the party. She couldn't help it, and that was too much for me. As we drove she kept rubbing on that black police ink mark on the back of her hand. We all had one. By the time we got home she had told me all of it, at least I think that was all of it. She had just been with him the day before he died. The day before, imagine. She said it had to be her fault. That's about how much sense it all made."

"I'm sorry, Drake. He was a destructive person, but I don't follow the logic of that, either."

"It made sense to her, that's all I know. After I brought her over to her sister's place I went through a bunch of things she'd thrown in our trash. I'm not normally that nosy but I was upset. Still am."

He reached into his shirt pocket and pulled out a photo. It showed a woman bent over on her knees, her wrists tied behind her bare back, and on its curve, I could've counted her vertebrae. Her hair was black but I couldn't identify her. The upper part of her panties was barely visible, a light gray and green stripe. "It's Pilar. I think he must have sent it to her some time ago."

"And Pilar getting this picture is what brought her back to him? Is that what you're saying?"

"From what I learned years ago, returning to

this kind of situation often needs a trigger. This could've been it. When I checked my email this morning I found the same photo addressed to me from Raul. The caption was, 'Now she's mine again.' It must have come in yesterday and I hadn't checked my messages before we went to the party."

A long moment of silence settled over us. In the garden Orlando had disappeared. He didn't handle this kind of information any better than I did. I could only recall the way Pilar and Drake had looked at each other at the party, years ago now, but less than twenty-four hours.

"What now, Drake? This is more your business than mine, but you wanted to keep me from thinking she killed him. Isn't that right?"

He shrugged. "Yes, or that I killed him, for beating her up. Naturally, I knew you'd be investigating this, if only to take the heat off Maya. I had to talk to you, can you see that?" For the first time he looked me in the face and his eyes welled up. His look said he had nowhere else to go with this.

I stood up and gripped his wrist. "Drake, please don't worry about me and what I might do here, or what I think. I appreciate that you told me this. Neither you nor Pilar is in my crosshairs." In a case with many potential suspects, none yet stood above the crowd. I hadn't worked anything out beyond that.

"But what should I do now? Do I talk to that other cop when he gets back? I just don't know."

"I would say nothing to Delgado. I don't think the other boarders will tell him anything about this, even if any of them know. If he does hear of it, I'll take him aside and tell him what you told me today, OK? He does listen to me some of the time."

"Sure, I can see why he would."

"And, if I can suggest it, you could do one more thing."

His eyebrows went up hopefully.

"Go see Pilar tonight. Tell her how much you love and value her. Show her there is more than one way to be a man, because, although she knows how to be a woman, she can still learn a different way to be *with* a man, a different kind of man. She must be acting out a lesson she learned a long time ago. Since Raul is gone, this is the right time to move on. You can still both help each other get through this and save something for yourselves."

The case was starting to look like a field of debris from the collapse of people's lives. Perhaps I would end up like Drake, sifting through their garbage. Well, we had done that before too. Sometimes it offers more information than any interrogation.

Wishing Cody could have heard his story, I stood in the doorway and watched Drake Wilson walk down to his Range Rover, his chest still heaving, and drive away with a small wave. I thought I had done both him and Pilar a favor, but I had to ask myself why it wasn't easier to act with that kind of insight at times in my own life with Maya.

Closing the front door and bolting it again, I wondered suddenly whether that had really been such a good insight after all. It may have been the right advice for their relationship, but had I given Pilar a pass she might not have deserved? It was the act of a nice guy, not a role I work at. While *Nice guys finish last* is not a phrase I connect with this business; the accurate phrase would be more like *Nice guys don't finish at all.*

Back in the great room I booted the computer and pulled up the file with the party photos. In the middle of the sequence was one I hadn't paid much attention to. Three people I scarcely knew were talking to each other. At the right edge of the frame, partially in the background, a solitary Drake Wilson stood framed by the French doors at the terrace and stared off toward the kitchen. One arm was raised and the back of his hand rested against his lips as if he were searching for someone he had lost in the crowd.

CHAPTER FIFTEEN
MAYA SANCHEZ

The day after Diego Delgado's return, and her and Cody's nearly immediate release from jail, Maya drove to Rancho Aria to talk with Phaedra Montgomery Kingman. As if the stain of humiliation and outrage could be removed with soap and hot water, a forty-five minute soak in the bathtub the evening before had washed her skin clean again, even if it still took Paul's extensive full body massage to reawaken all her dormant nerve endings. An hour in bed was followed by grilled giant shrimp wrapped in bacon, asparagus on the side, and a Caesar salad, served with an elegant white Burgundy they'd received as a gift from a satisfied client.

"Jail is the death of the mind," she said to Paul as she worked on her second glass, but still with a recovering smile. "It's a way of becoming trash, *basura*. You are nothing more than a thing in a box with bars on it. You have no privacy, and you have to eat the garbage they feed you or starve."

Maya had put this out of her mind, as she first spent time brushing Martina, a way of reconnecting after her jail experience before it was time to go up to the house, on duty again. The firm set to her jaw suggested how ready she was to advance this case, if only as a way of striking back. It was not the first case where the official law enforcement team had stood in their way.

Maya washed her hands and wiped them carefully so she didn't smell like horse after she left Martina's stall before approaching the house. She had a history of interrogating formidable women for the Agency (to say nothing of softening up even more self-important men), so she felt no nervousness. It was late in the morning on a Wednesday, and Luis, the houseboy, showed Maya out onto the broad rear terrace at the east side of the house. The canopy was gone and the eight unused dining tables had been placed back in storage. The sun was brilliant, and if any threat of rain was assembling a later appearance, it was still elsewhere out gathering support.

Seated under an expansive canvas umbrella, Phaedra awaited her at the circular marble table in the center. Next to her rested a Japan lacquer tray offering coffee, tea, milk, sugar, with an assortment of low-calorie wafers. When Maya approached, Phaedra did not rise, although she offered both hands. She was wearing an exquisitely embroidered peasant top and skirt that no peasant in México could have dreamed of affording.

"I want to thank you, dear, for coming out here to help us clear up this horrible staff problem. Having a murder occur in one's own home, even in a remote service area, is simply so *vulgar* I can scarcely bear to think about it. One feels like having all the rugs cleaned." She fanned herself briefly, although the mid morning air was still cool. "Here in México, of course, one can *never* find staff of the proper class. That, I feel, is somehow at the root of this problem. After all, at the end of the day, isn't it all about selection and proper training?" Phaedra's unmerited agony still shadowed her face.

"I feel the same way," Maya said, with no idea at all what Phaedra meant. To her, staff in México, which she had grown up with in the capital, had only a single class: staff. "Has Raul's funeral been held yet?" She had heard no announcements.

"I really wouldn't know. I assumed it would be held somewhere in the campo, if it has. That's a place I avoid whenever possible."

After all, Maya thought, the campo includes only 98% of México. "I can't imagine what you're going to do now for a trainer." Although this was not the point of Maya's visit, it was of critical interest to her as a boarder.

"That, like anything else beyond the limits of this house where we're sitting, will be the duty of Max to solve." As if that was the end of it, she beckoned to Luis to pour the tea or coffee.

"I'm sure he will."

"He simply must. I presume you're here in your capacity as some part of the Paul Zacher Agency staff." Her wrist twitched slightly as if she were unsure which part that was. This move masked a covert glance at her watch that did not escape Maya.

"Of course. Otherwise I wouldn't be wasting your time. I'm the chief executive officer, that part of the staff."

"Ah! But I assumed that would have to be your husband."

"So did he at the beginning." Maya felt no need to mention they weren't married.

A moment of silence fell over the table. Designed to accommodate eight with ample elbowroom, it was five and a half feet across, so the awkward gulf separating just two people felt like a confrontation. With a gesture of high refinement, Phaedra helped herself to a virginal pair of wafers and followed with a modest sip of her tea. Maya waited, both hands gripping her coffee cup, wondering where Max might be hiding. Could he be watching this? Being able to walk was one thing, but could he participate in a conversation that did not accommodate his social rank, his wealth, and his lifelong deception?

"Out on the grounds I've heard some talk about Raul's relationship with the women here." Maya waited to say this until Phaedra had swallowed. Paul had brought her up to date on his conversation with Drake Wilson. She had at first attempted to explain Pilar's inclinations to him, but then realized she didn't fully understand them herself.

"Raul may have misbehaved among the staff, but not the boarders, I'm quite certain. I think one listens to such idle talk at one's own peril."

"As an investigator I've learned to thrive on peril. Without it, you discover nothing. I've felt Raul's hands on me too, even as hard as I tried to look like a boarder. Perhaps he mistook me for staff."

Phaedra paused with her cup halfway to her lips again. She looked unsure of whether she had been fully able to veil her response to this. "And I suppose you are now here on a voyage of discovery, much like Cortés."

"More like the Inquisition. That's how I pay for my board." We are only fencing, Maya thought. Now I wish I had a facemask. At some point I will need to draw some real blood, and that moment is not far off. After that, there will be a sudden thrust at my eyes.

"I understand there was a pregnancy here last year." Maya had picked up this news in the paddock one morning, listening to the grooms, who tended to think no one among the boarders was fluent in Spanish.

"Well, yes, and we did send that girl off to Mexico City in a private car for an abortion. It was the least we could do for her."

"And was Raul responsible for her condition?"

Phaedra shifted in her chair. "Let me say only that we preferred discretion to an investigation. Neither Max nor I cared to pursue a matter that was so clearly painful to the staff. Such things happen here, as you must know. As a woman, I decided that our most important role was being supportive to that girl. After all, we are to some degree the patrons here and we must take it upon ourselves to act in that manner. Max and I have always been prepared to acknowledge the responsibilities of our rank and class."

"You chose to be an example to others."

"Exactly. I'm pleased that you understand that. So many people feel that if one is born into some small degree of privilege one can simply drift through society unconcerned about others. That, however, has never been our style."

"So then, with the same perspective, if Raul had been involved with one or even several of the boarders, you would find it necessary to make the same response, or at least to offer that option?"

"To send them off to the capital for a procedure? I hardly think we would go that far." She pretended to laugh.

Abortion is illegal in the state of Guanajuato and more than half the other states in México. Women without means can rarely afford the journey to Mexico City for a legal one.

"Do you think that Raul's death might in some way be connected to his philandering here at Rancho Aria?"

Phaedra peered at her for a moment as if the air had suddenly thickened between them, resulting in a corresponding degree of blur in their communication. "And has that been established with any degree of certainty?"

"We can take a survey and generate a number. I would be happy to start with the other boarders. The three men in that group we can write off."

Before Maya had finished this sentence she noticed a slight lateral movement in Phaedra's left wrist. While it may have been a nervous tick, it may also have been something else more germane. Luis, the houseboy, came trotting out with a cellphone in his hand.

"I am so sorry to interrupt, Señora, but here is a most important call, the one you have been waiting for."

With a deep sigh, Phaedra shrugged as she turned to Maya. "I simply must take this. It's about an urgent family problem at home. I do hope, though, that we can resume this discussion at another time." She rose and turned away toward the hills in the east before Maya had a chance to get up, as if facing England would make her voice clearer to the other party.

If there was another party.

Maya's own cell went off as she approached the parking corral feeling cut off at the knees, although she'd had no great hope of getting very far on this subject with Phaedra. Cody was on the other end. He had been getting background checks done on Max, Phaedra, and some of the boarders through his longstanding connections in the Chicago Police. Phaedra's had taken a bit longer since it had to go through secondary contacts in London. Max had come up clear, although some minor banking regulation issues with two other family members had surfaced. Max himself had never worked at the family bank because of his disabled condition. Drake's record bore no black marks.

"I've got some background information on Phaedra, and I thought I'd give it to you directly, since I know you're going to talk to her."

"I just finished, and sooner than I expected."

"Well, even so, you'll find this interesting. Plug it into what you already found out from her. Phaedra's real name is Thelma Mae Perkins. She was born in the East End of London, in one of the poorest of neighborhoods. At sixteen she won a beauty contest sponsored by a cosmetics company, followed with three magazine ads for them, and out of that she snagged a scholarship to acting school."

"And she's been onstage ever since."

"Exactly, although I guess her career was begin

ning to falter when Max appeared to rescue her. She was thirty-six then. It appears that she has always had a knack for landing on her feet."

"As always, timing matters. We'll see how far it can take her now."

CHAPTER SIXTEEN

Work often gets tedious, and that's why some people play golf. Detectives more often tend to party, at least at the Paul Zacher Agency. That evening the occasion was a reunion on Quebrada. We were determined to celebrate Cody and Maya's release from jail because of Diego Delgado's intervention. He was not embarrassed when all three of us hugged him at the door; after all, he was Mexican. We could've carried him inside bouncing on our shoulders. Such displays are allowed here. Maya's hug, warm and intimate, was clearly his favorite response.

For the first time in the Agency's history, we had invited Diego Delgado to dinner. As an event focused on police business, we had not asked his wife, whom none of us had ever met. He told us she had gone along to the convention in Guadalajara, and was now happy to stay home and settle back in. Crime was not her life.

As we sat in the great room, the new bottle of Herradura Añejo tequila was prominent on a silver tray on the end table next to where we seated Delgado. The unused portion would go home with him. Cody stood, raised and extended his planter's punch, and Maya and I lifted our glasses too as we rose to our feet.

"Back in the homicide division in Illinois when a guy came through for you in a tight spot we all stood up and called him a *mensch*. That only means a man in German, but in the highest sense, and not every male person measures up to that level by a long shot. Here's to you, Licenciado Delgado!" Cody flushed. This was a bit out of his normal range, which tended more toward flexing fingers and lifting eyelids to measure rigor mortis.

During the chatter that followed I thought about Según's remarks about bias and premium tequila shooters at our house. A lot depends on nomenclature, and I prefer to call it a partnership. This was our fourteenth case, and Delgado's help had often been vital in getting things done. Too much objectivity can get in the way of that. The rulebook cannot solve everything, since heart, connections, and intuition matter more in this business than many would like to admit. Delgado rose and offered another toast focused on how the Zacher Agency had raised the quality of the gringo community in San Miguel. I could see that Maya wasn't sure how to take this. Perhaps she was an honorary *gringa*.

"Licenciado Según will be absent to attend a sensitivity workshop in México for a while, starting next week," Delgado said. "México" is commonly used by natives to indicate the capital city, the same way we leave the D.C. off Washington back in the States. "He may be gone for a few months of intensive training. Sometimes these courses must be repeated to have their full effect on slow learners."

"Yet we did not find him lacking in ambition," I said, "even though when I talked with him he was not actually sitting at your desk."

"No, we have given him high marks there, but that is not everything to consider, as you know."

I refilled his shooter. We had agreed earlier that we wouldn't reveal Max's secret yet. I was eager to see what Delgado had come up with in his case review. He did want to hear more detail about Maya's encounter with Raul earlier on the day of the murder. So did I. She had been gone at Rancho Aria much of that day and we had never spoken about it.

She told the story starting from her entry into the tack room that morning. The outcome did not surprise me, and I was happy to see the injuries on Raul's back harmlessly explained.

"At what point did you encounter Señorita Bontemps?" said Delgado.

"Is that her name? Now I understand. Now it comes together." She looked at me.

"She was the witness that morning?" I said. "Is that what you mean? Licenciado Según wouldn't give me the name."

"Of course," Delgado said. "The only serious witness we have so far, but the wounds match the saddle rack in the tack room. Raul Sanchez has been buried, but we have the measurements and the shape of the injuries from the autopsy. This is why we are all sitting here tonight. As for Señor Williams' outburst at the arrest, it was within my discretion to dismiss that as simple enthusiasm in protecting a woman he knew to be innocent."

Maya was still staring at me.

"Might've been worse," I said with a shrug. "Renée could have said she heard you swear you would kill Raul with an ice pick the first chance you had."

"The same Renée? This may be getting too complicated," Cody said. "I need another drink."

Maya rose to make him another planter's punch.

"That's how witnesses are," I said. "You know it too."

"They must always be taken with a squeeze of lime," said Delgado.

"Like a grain of salt. So now we are in the clear." Even if we hadn't been, it was where I wished to be. "But who killed Raul Sanchez?"

Delgado raised both hands as if to deny his own involvement. "For myself, I have an alibi from being in the presence of 281 other police officers that evening. In the absence of any witnesses at the party, which we are not certain of yet, we have only the physical evidence. Because of its rough surface, the ice pick has no fingerprints, and the angle of penetration is worthless because the fatal strike was second and the victim would have bent over to escape after the first, which was too shallow to measure the angle properly."

Maya brought out some spicy starters and Cody was already pacing back and forth, the only mannerism he had that reminded me of Sherlock Holmes.

"Does the strike from the back suggest a woman?" I asked. "A person who could not face a forceful retaliation from the front by the victim? The ice pick could've been thrust through his rib cage into his heart and had the same effect."

"Such a thing is possible. We also know that the ice pick belonged to the house, rather than being brought in. The unusual handle was carved by the son of the cook, Ofelia, with his small pocketknife. He works for the property, mostly on the grounds. He is not, as we would say, quite right in the head, so the *familia* Kingman tries to make him busy to pay him some nominal amount. Otherwise Ofelia would have to keep at home with him, and they enjoy her services as a cook. It works out the best for everyone."

Possibly, I thought, wondering if Raul might have offered some insult to Ofelia and the son had heard it. As we had recently learned in another case, unsophisticated people kill as easily as anyone else, and this looked to me like an impulse murder, given the weapon. Of course, that motive seemed too light for a murder, and Raul must have had dozens of enemies.

"I have often seen him there by the house when I come to ride," said Maya. "His name is Ivan." She pronounced it like Yvonne. I had seen him too on one occasion, holding a bag for other workers loading yard waste. He looked benign and harmless, if a little vague.

"Is there a mental health problem with him?" said Cody, pausing. "Or is he only retarded, as we used to say in the States? Not that it was any bed of roses. I'm not sure what it's called up there now, I've been down here too long."

"We can look at that. But for now, offering no threats, Ivan goes nowhere, I think, but home with his mother at the end of the day." A subtle mellowness had overtaken Delgado by degrees. If this was his new broadcast frequency, the rest of us were ready to receive this wavelength.

"How old is he?"

"Mid forties. But I want to think deeper on this." His hands waved aside the surface debris, some of which was subtly gathering on the coffee table before him, a few Spanish peanut husks and a damp napkin. I came over to clean up as he talked. "We are seeing some possible layers of motive here, even as we start to look at all the party guests and all the boarders. And the staff is not free of suspicion. I will give you my impressions later."

"It's a large field," said Cody.

Here Delgado's hand, gripping the empty shooter, seemed to tremble, as if from a fear that going on without a refill might suggest the wrong impression to less seasoned investigators. Cody reloaded him this time, as one cop to another.

"I will try to gain access for a moment to my emotional layers. It is a complicated case."

"Oh God," said Maya, an entity she had never before addressed in my presence, nor, as I knew, was it one she ever planned to meet.

Maintaining a marginal sanity as the host on occasions like this is my long suit, so I went out to the garden to light the barbecue, which was ready for my match. When I returned they were only getting into it further.

"…as much as Señorita Diana Freeman, I think," Delgado was saying. "When I spoke to her on the second round she was very nervous."

"But she's so young," Maya said. "I'm sure she's never been involved in a murder before and it's too much for her to handle."

"Well, that may not be the case." A sly smile came over Delgado's face. "She formerly boarded at a stable in Querétaro, near where her family lives. Her father is in the auto manufacturing business."

"And?" I said.

"A young man died there, close to her in age. He

had been beaten badly when he was found and he did not regain consciousness or survive his injuries. She left home shortly after and came to San Miguel by her own to live here."

"No arrests?" said Cody.

"No."

"I have studied her…" I said.

"Of course," Maya interrupted, "as you would anyone."

"…and I don't think she is constructed in a way that she could beat up some guy to the point where he died of his injuries. She's, well, lightly made. She wouldn't get through a typical man's defenses on a frontal attack."

"So then she might attack from behind, as with Raul's killer," said Cody. "Just thinking now how this might have gone."

"The real question," said Maya, "is what her relationship was with Raul."

"But did he have any actual relationships?" I said. "Or were they merely liaisons? Who was really connected with him?"

This train of thought reminded me of Según's case against Maya. It was constructed from cobwebs and sawdust.

It crossed my mind to bring up Drake and Pilar, but after the way we parted it didn't seem right. Still, this reunion had turned into an examination of the possible suspects, at least the ones presently visible. After a while spent going farther down the list, including any grooms that might hate Raul, the garbage collectors who had been yelled at, two women boarders who had left in disgust—we could get this list from Max—husbands of women unconnected to Rancho Aria that Raul may have been involved with on his own time, and even the household staff. I went out to the loggia and threw the fajita fixings on the grill. This committed me to remain with them, flipping them around, for about ten minutes. Maya departed for the kitchen to prepare the tortillas and salsas. Delgado and Cody stayed on the case.

During dinner in the loggia I became increasingly convinced that Delgado needed to know about Max's forty-five year ruse. He might be able to connect it with information he hadn't shared with us, and I never thought he told us everything.

"What's your take on Max Kingman?" I asked him during a lull. His hand paused lifting a spoonful of Maya's lethal *serrano* salsa onto his fajita.

"He is a man, I would think, who knows what he wants and is not afraid to say it. By his own story, he would have been the greatest of the riders at Rancho Aria. A truly historic figure which destiny has cheated him of being."

"By his own story."

"His own story is often the only one allowed."

"And the Señora Kingman?" Cody asked.

"She too will have her own story, but sometimes not the same as his."

"Are either of them suspects in this?" said Maya.

"The Señora may be, but Señor Max is unlikely."

The rest of us looked at each other in silence.

"Did you spend much time with him?" From his look, I wondered whether Delgado was beginning to pick up something about Max from us. A long moment passed before he answered, placing his elbows on the table and touching his fingertips together.

"Perhaps it is not enough, as I am thinking now, only about half an hour. Are you proposing we visit him together? I have heard your powers of interrogation can be most formidable."

Even if unconventional, I thought.

CHAPTER SEVENTEEN

W hat we proposed was indeed a joint venture. For Diego Delgado and the Judicial Police to work directly with a civilian detective agency was highly unusual, but we had done it before, even if rarely. Convincing him that Max knew more than he was telling us was not difficult, even if we weren't sure what it was, beyond the obvious (to us) faking of his disability. We also weren't sure what would happen during this encounter, but the pitch we made to Delgado was that the combination of four of us could set off a reaction. Sometimes this kind of detective work is about nothing more sophisticated than getting in people's faces and watching what happens.

Delgado regarded this as an important case. Max's status guaranteed that the eyes of the expat community would be on how he handled it. Many of the equestrian expats were quite well heeled and had voices that could be heard as far away as city hall. A conviction in Raul's murder would elevate Delgado's status in both communities.

We could simply have told him what we knew about Max's mobility, but if Max laughed at that as a crude and tasteless joke, what could we prove? Any man who had spent forty-five years in a wheelchair would automatically get the benefit of the doubt. To suggest he was really mobile would get us laughed off the stage by every other player in this little drama. The idea that anyone would choose to be so self-limiting would never sell.

Maya and I had gone through Max's condition in detail with Cody, our staff psychologist. He felt much the same as Amanda Klein did. It was a massive failure of nerve that had come on at a time when Max must have first realized there were some things he could only do for himself. In response, he had chosen to become a connoisseur who was never subjected to being tested again. We had heard people say that failure was not an option. In this case it was the same, but only because testing was not an option.

The four of us now stood on the long front porch of the house at Rancho Aria, accompanied by two uniformed cops waiting on the step below who came with us to reinforce, I thought, the image of our official presence by bringing the total to fifty percent real police.

Zzzt!

The houseboy came to the door to lead us to Max's bedroom. None of us had seen it but Maya during her shoe expedition, and she had suggested it was worth a look, filled as it was with awards and photos from Max's riding days. When Delgado set up the interview he stressed that we especially wished to survey the small loggia off the bedroom that had a view of the paddock, and more distantly, the ring and the jumps beyond. Max expressed no difficulty about this, even when he was informed that the Paul Zacher Agency would be coming with Delgado.

Empty of party guests, and with the blinds pulled on the French doors overlooking the rear terrace to screen out the morning light, the huge great room with its classic art, lived-in furniture and carpets looked strangely innocent. It came off better filled with partygoers, humming with chatter. Even with the six of us standing there it felt empty.

"We are like invaders now," Maya said softly. "The Señora must have her private place too, not in this grand room."

How could we be there for a murder investigation when everything around us spoke of the seasoned good taste of several generations? When we entered Max's bedroom Phaedra was there to greet us too. She was dressed in a rose-colored pajama-like ensemble that looked formal enough to wear entertaining a brunch party, although her hair was wrapped in a stylish turban that suggested her hairdresser had not yet appeared. Cody and Phaedra were the only ones who needed an introduction. Laszlo was not present. Phaedra barely acknowledged any of us.

"We are so grateful that you are able to take this appointment for us today," said Delgado, stepping forward with an air of cooperation. "It is only that we find several details to clear up and I'm sure it will not require much of your time."

"I wasn't goin' anywhere," said Max with a shrug. He needed a shave. If the hair on his head had become thinner without retreating in area, the shadow of his beard was still dense. Ten o'clock may have been a bit too early in his day for a meeting like this. The unspoken suggestion was that Laszlo was necessary to get him up and functioning.

At the front wall of the house the bedroom had a high round window to admit the afternoon sun. Beneath it was a queen-size bed. To the right as we faced it, the long wall over the paddock and ring looked north, and next to Max's desk a set of French doors opened onto the loggia. Above the desk it was all glass. Around the corner was a wood-burning fireplace with a carved stone mantel. On the fourth wall, along the inner corridor, were two closets and Max's bathroom. One of these closets held the telltale shoes.

"Here you see," said Phaedra, her arms extended toward the windows, "Max's eagle's nest. This is what keeps him at the top of his form. It sustains his engagement."

"Your past is so much present here," I said, scanning the mantel with a courteous wave. The carved limestone displayed a diverse collection of two-handled cups and engraved crystal tablet awards artfully arranged. "There must be fifteen of them."

"Seventeen," he said drily. He was seated with his back to the bathroom door, facing out over his desk across the room. To his right, beyond the last closet door, a long hall table exhibited dozens of photos, mostly dressage shots, none of them of jumpers, and a few of personalities he must have known. Above this display hung a portrait of a young man. The curious blue eyes told me it was the youthful Max Kingman. While the face was vigorous and handsome, it also included a hint of self-indulgence that his great uncle Alistair's lacked.

"I wonder if you have ever witnessed anything down in the paddock from this viewpoint that would suggest Raul might have abused a boarder or was misusing his position in some other way?" Delgado waited politely for him to respond.

Max shook his head slowly. "I tended not to watch him much. Instead I observed the boarders themselves. I liked to assess their progress, or their lack of it." He gave Maya a pale smile. "You've been doing much better lately, of course."

I wasn't listening as they chatted about the finer points of riding, instead I drifted closer to the photos, bending over to catch the detail. From his seated position Max would've been able to see them from a better angle. In the middle of the group was an autographed one of George Bush as Governor of Texas. It was inscribed to Max. I felt his eyes follow me as I turned to examine the trophies on the mantel next.

Cody stood on the other side of the ranch owner, closer to the bed, not far away and watching in silence. I had told him what was going to happen and he was ready, his hands loose at his sides, his fingers flexing slightly as if about to go for his gun with no warning. Of course, he hadn't worn one.

"I'd forgotten how inviting this room is in the morning," Phaedra said, as if about to serve tea. She crossed to the windows.

"A stunning group of trophies," I said, shaking my head as if amazed. Some were engraved silver cups showing no tarnish, others were crystal in various configurations, and two were bronze horse figures on bases of exotic wood, each fronted by a brass plaque. There was not a speck of dust on any of them. "This must be your favorite." In the center stood a crystal plaque with frosted edges and an engraved legend beneath the etched head of a horse with mane flying. I reached out and casually picked it up as if it were only a dime store trinket.

"Wait there! Hey, wait a minute! Be careful! You're going to leave your prints on that!" A sharp note of panic rang out in Max's voice. I was sure that no visitor was ever allowed to touch these. He may have dusted them himself. We had reached the holy of holies, the tabernacle where Max enshrined his past.

"Don't worry," I said, with a casual wave. "I'm known for my excellent grip. Watch." I released both hands from the trophy, and as it accelerated toward the tiled floor, I bent and caught it at my knees. I suddenly enjoyed playing the careless bumpkin.

"Stop that, goddamn it! Put that thing back right now!" Max's hands gripped the armrests of his wheelchair. His eyes held mine as a silence born of deeply anxious anticipation blanketed the room. Although I looked at no one but Max, from the corner of my eye I caught the painfully embarrassed expression that distorted Delgado's features. His arms came up like those of a referee, as if to wave me away from the mantel, even from the room, or the house itself.

I held the crystal tablet high with one hand and swung it downward behind me in an arc. As it rose again, I lofted it into the air on a course to pass about six feet in front of Max Kingman.

His mouth gaping in terror, like a prisoner unbound, with a strangled yelp he surged up and outward, intercepting the trophy at full arm's length, then clutched it to his breast, bowing his head over it. Even his chin clamped it against his collarbone. Max was left standing there motionless, several steps out from his wheelchair, which, from the force of his exit, rolled slowly backward until it tapped the bathroom door, the only sound in the bedroom.

"You ridiculous old fool!" hissed Phaedra, and swept out through the door.

Maya had turned away. Delgado stood there frozen like a man caught in a trap. The silence was as heavy as damask curtains.

Maya was next to leave the room, shaking her head. Cody edged closer to Max, leaned into his space, where the man had still not moved, perhaps paralyzed now for the first time in his life. Cody said, "*Zzzt!*" in perfect imitation of the front porch bug zapper.

I followed him out with Delgado muttering behind me.

In the late afternoon, Cody stopped by for a self-congratulatory cognac, saying he was going to meet Sheila, his girlfriend, later. After he left, Maya and I opened a bottle of our best Chilean wine and skipped dinner for a batch of *totopos* and salsa. We both felt we'd been through an emotional crescendo, even if it wasn't our own. We talked about the obvious; where Max would go from here.

"You didn't tell me you were going to do that." We were lying in bed later, not quite ready to sleep. This was often the time for conversations like this. I thought of them as off the record, things we wouldn't share with Cody.

"No." I shook my head slowly. "I wasn't sure I could pull it off. It depended on where Max was sitting and where Cody was standing. I had to be by the mantel. But I'd been thinking about it ever since you described all the trophies he had, particularly the crystal ones. How far would he go to protect one? If they were awards he'd won himself and he'd revered them for years, if they defined who he was or had been, he might not think before he jumped out of character."

She was lying on her side facing me, her head supported on one arm. With two fingers I lifted a long lock of hair off her cheek. She was wearing a thin pale blue cotton nightshirt that came to about mid thigh. Her fine skin was always a marvel to me. The only lamp we had on was the reading light behind her head. It left her face in shadow, but her eyes were eloquent. "But Cody was ready. I could see from his hands that he was expecting something."

"I told him to be prepared to catch the trophy if Max missed it. That was all."

Far away a siren began to wail and two dogs outside picked up the melody until it faded.

"I think you enjoyed doing that," she said.

"I guess I did, although I had to think about it too. The tipping point was that I owed it to Delgado after he released you and Cody. Otherwise, I was asking myself why it should be my job to unmask Max, after a lifetime of deception. Usually I'm not big on intervention, and I'm happy to let people believe what they need to believe. We all have our illusions, don't we?"

"It was a lifetime of being superior to people trying to do what he wouldn't try to do himself. Besides, it's a murder case, a time when the masks have to come off."

"Do you really think that?"

Nodding, she put her hand on my cheek. "I'm starting to see what was bothering me all along. It's that nothing is what it seems at Rancho Aria, or very little is. I don't know how I sensed that. Every time you take a close look at something the edges become all fuzzy and it turns into something else."

"I can see that. But you were the first one to pick up on it."

"It's going to cost me too. I don't know if Martina and I will be able to stay there. Raul's death was bad enough, but revealing Max's lie will destabilize the rancho even more than just the loss of a good trainer.

Who knows who Max will become now that he's walking around upright like the rest of us?"

"Like a real person? Then he'll just have to reinvent himself, won't he?"

"Yes, like the rest of us do from time to time. Welcome home, darling. I think you've moved on from the fire and now you're back to work."

She reached up and turned out the light.

I didn't suggest to Maya as she nestled in beside me that the next phase of being back to work was to find out who Raul Sanchez really was.

CHAPTER EIGHTEEN
CODY WILLIAMS

As a person recently freed from jail, but not entirely freed of bitterness, Cody lost no time in committing his next felony that afternoon, following the trophy toss in Max's bedroom and the celebratory cognac at Paul's house. He had some time before he was to meet Sheila.

For a mere 100 pesos he had persuaded Carlos, the Rancho Aria entrance guard, to give him the home address of Raul Sanchez. Carlos maintained a current directory of everyone who worked or boarded there, along with the make and model of their car and the license number. For visitors whose names were not on that list, he collected their driver's licenses and held them during their visit.

Cody's pretext in asking was that he wanted to leave a small memorial of flowers and a sympathy card at the dead man's door, where he knew for certain, he said, there must already be many others. He acknowledged that he was not yet a rider, but having seen the miraculous improvement Raul had accomplished for Maya, he had been planning to start lessons soon when word of Raul's tragic death reached him. Now he was saddened and confused.

"Of course," said Carlos, touched that this huge American, six-foot-three and 230 pounds, could have a heart so perfectly in proportion to his frame. In his experience, not many gringos did, most possessing only a puny emotional life. Carlos himself had been working that day, but he had already heard that Señora Montgomery had not attended the funeral, either. Señor Max, as a disabled person, was not expected to, even though he owned a white Suburban adapted for wheelchair travelers. It even had a little power lift on the passenger side. Carlos had observed it in action on the day the vehicle was delivered.

As a courtesy, Cody had shown Carlos a draft of the message he intended to leave at Raul's house, asking him to check the spelling and grammar. Carlos made only one small change, from the familiar to the formal, given the solemnity of the occasion and the fact that Cody had never met Raul alive.

Cody drove off thinking about the episode in Max's bedroom. He had never forgotten the psychology training that had nearly gotten him a Ph.D., and the trophy episode had confirmed what he earlier thought he was looking at in Max Kingman. He saw Max's highly principled view of riding skills as the need to be merely judgmental in order to feel superior to other riders. He also found Max's self-righteousness repulsive.

None of this, however, led him to think Max had killed Raul, even though Cody suspected that was exactly where Delgado was going to go with his new information. Perhaps Max would end up spending some time in the *carcel* himself. Cody knew of at least one empty cell available there now.

Driving in off the road to Dolores Hidalgo, a few minutes later Cody approached Raul's house. It was possible that his family had already cleared the place out, but Cody knew that things move at their own pace in México, and the relatives, burdened with deep mourning, would've quickly come by to clear out the cash and jewelry, while they waited for a less emotional period to hold the sale of routine household goods. Raul's cousin had already driven away from the rancho in the two-year-old pickup. They could sort out later who might actually inherit it. Cody couldn't imagine that the trainer had ever filed a will.

Certainly Raul's mattress had seen a lot of hard use and would not fetch much, even when cleaned. Because of metal fatigue, bedsprings have a finite lifespan, and the neighbors nearest to his open windows would know that better than many others who lived at a greater distance.

Cody's lock picks, somewhat worn after years of application in México, were still well tuned to the cheap local hardware, which demanded little precision. He was inside Raul's house in less than thirty seconds. It was a three-room affair on the edge of the pilgrimage village of Atotonilco. The windowless façades on both sides were similar and anonymous. The two small wilted clutches of posies lying flattened on the step confirmed he was in the right place. No grieving notes were attached.

Inside, the light switch on the front wall ignored his repeated touch. The power, always a pricy item, had already been shut down. Cody closed the door softly at his back and pulled out his flashlight. Initially it picked out a cheap paper image of the Virgin of Guada- lupe on the opposite wall. Fastened to the plaster with blue pushpins, the frayed corners curled back in the humidity. Cody thought this might be the only virgin to have remained in the house for any length of time.

The single piece of furniture that stood out in the room was a black leather lounger, the tufted throne of the master, facing a large flat screen television. The remote was ready at one side on a stone pedestal. Raul's women friends could sit on a worn floral love seat at the side. In one corner a small square wooden table would've seated four, had there been more than two chairs. No books were in view, and no other art graced the walls. A fine coating of dust covered everything. Cody decided that Phaedra would've met Raul elsewhere for their trysts. He recalled Maya saying Phaedra had not attended the funeral. Either she didn't forgive him for being murdered or she had done it herself.

In the kitchen, the refrigerator had been emptied, and the cupboards were bare. The bedroom lay beyond, a small room mostly taken up with a queen-sized bed. A pair of windows opened to an untended courtyard beyond.

The nightstand held a pair of reading glasses, tissue, lubricants and condoms, two pornographic magazines and a set of six unlabeled keys. A small bathroom with a shower, sink, and stool took up one corner, with a closet next to it, and in the recess beyond, a bare metal desk with a lamp mounted on the wall above it. He pulled open the drawer to find an inexpensive Toshiba laptop several years old. Here was a crossroads. If the motive for Raul's murder was something other than his philandering, that information might be on the computer. Cody did not think Delgado's people would investigate Raul in the matter of his own murder, so he decided to take it with him. The house offered nothing else of interest. If Raul had discovered the means of profiting from his job beyond his salary, the place showed no sign of it.

He opened the front door a few inches and looked into the street. Nothing moved. Cody drove away with the laptop on the floor beside him. It could be returned to the family later as if it had been discovered at the rancho. If it contained valuable evidence, he would turn it over to Diego Delgado.

CHAPTER NINETEEN

Raul Sanchez' cheap laptop had no password to keep us from exploring his files. That might've been a measure of his arrogance, or simple carelessness. Cody and Maya and I sat in the great room later that day in front of the enclosed Spanish colonial style desk we'd had made to conceal our own computer and business files. Our house doesn't have an office, and we prefer to keep the second bedroom for guests. My large painting studio takes up the rest of the second floor. We pulled in two straight-back chairs from the dining room for extra seating, and made ourselves ready, if not fully comfortable at what might be coming.

This was not the first computer we'd cracked into that didn't belong to us. People always think their files are like the inside of their own mind, a perfectly private and secure place, that short of torture, no one can invade. The truth is you don't have to be the Chinese government to get into these pools of poorly secured information. On an earlier case we'd used our website designer to crack the password on a different computer. It took him less than half a day.

Raul's desktop image offered a shot of Mádrigal running free in the ring, his nose in the air, possibly sniffing out the scent of a mare in heat. None of us commented. Cody's finger reached out and touched an icon labeled *Los Entretenimientos,* Pastimes.

It held many dozens of files by name: Susan, Rebecca, Dawn, Sylvia, Lenore, Kathryn, Rita, and so on. A last name initial was provided when a first name was duplicated. One file off to the side by itself was called, *Master List.*

"I don't see a file for you here," said Cody, grinning at Maya.

She gave him an elbow in the ribs. "He hadn't gotten to it yet."

"But I see one titled Phaedra," I said. "But rather than going for friends and family, let's arrange them in order of most recent use."

What we found was Diana, Pilar, Sophia, and Luisa as the top four.

"Diana I can see," said Maya, "but Pilar, I know you said she was hooked up with him and it was kinky, but even so…"

"Do you know a Sofia or Luisa?" said Cody.

"No, but I'm sure he's not only working his charms at the rancho."

I opened the Master List file and scrolled to the bottom of a database that contained 431 names. Cody and I both groaned. Maya covered her mouth in astonishment.

"Try to remember that he's probably been at this for twenty-five years," I said. Here, at least, was contact information for all four of our recent contenders, as well as everyone else. Scrolling down to Sophia we passed the spot where Renée would've been if she had made the list. Nor was Amanda Klein in place near the top.

"I'm going to look at a couple of the files, just to get a sense of it."

"You know what's going to be in them," Maya said.

"Most likely." I opened the Diana file. It contained pages of photos.

"Pretty tame," said Cody, his eyebrows going up in surprise. The first few were underwear shots. "I assumed these would all be nudes."

"Victoria's Secret, though," Maya said. "High end stuff."

In an amateurish way it was attractive, because Diana's look was trim and athletic, her skin fine, but she seemed only marginally into it. Her expression said, Just playing along. I was also surprised the shots weren't more revealing.

In the next set she seemed asleep, but on closer

look, her eyes were not fully shut. Her mouth was also partly open, but that didn't necessarily mean anything. The frame took in her body from the shoulders up. They were bare, but gave no more information. In total, this series contained six shots, all taken of her face from different angles. The detail was minuscule, even to the fine down of her upper lip, the pores on the shallow inward curve of her nose, the network of lines on her lips. You could count each single hair in her eyebrows. It was like looking at a scientific study of an insect pinned to a laboratory card.

"I don't like the looks of this at all," said Cody. "That girl is drugged."

Instead of being the subject of the photos, Diana seemed to be an object, merely that. I had been expecting robust, athletic mating games from these files, but this appeared to be something more sinister. Instead of telling a story of recreational sex marathons, they belonged more to a case study. If I had been feeling much sympathy for Raul's death, it had mostly evaporated by then.

"Get the contact information on those four and shut it down," said Maya. "This is sick."

I didn't bother with Pilar, thinking I'd find no surprises there after the photo Drake showed me, and we could always go back to it. He could give me her new contact info if we needed to talk to her.

Sofia provided a series of nudes that did not rise above raunchy in tone. I did not recognize her from her face, which appeared in few of the shots.

Finally, there was Luisa. A Mexican woman, as was Sofia, she was always fully clothed and shown in public. Some views showed her in the *jardín* reading, others walking up to the entrance of the Parroquia dressed as if for mass, and shopping at the Mega supermarket reading package labels. In none of them did she display any awareness of his presence.

"He's stalking her," Cody said. "She would've been his next conquest."

"This is probably the same as the opening to the lab shots of Diana," said Maya. "Here is the subject of the coming experiment in her natural habitat before the net fell on her."

We decided we didn't want to keep Raul's machine any longer. I hooked up a hard drive to the laptop and started a download of the entire set of files. Cody could replace it in his house tomorrow.

Later, we adjourned to the loggia with the brandy bottle. The sun had dropped beneath the rim of the west wall of the garden, leaving a lingering glow on the stone parapet. Orlando was somewhere up in the treetops settling in; we never knew exactly where he liked to spend the night. He may have been like Raul in that respect.

I had whipped up a batch of guacamole

earlier so we had something to munch on as an aid to deep thought.

"I don't think we need to talk to Luisa or Sofia," said Cody, scooping one of the big triangular chips into it. "Luisa would only be startled and uncomfortable to learn she was being stalked like that. We don't always enjoy hearing about our close escapes, either."

"I wonder if Diana is involved in this somehow," said Maya. "She may have seen those photos of herself unconscious and wondered what went on."

"You both saw her in the party photos. She and Raul were having some kind of disagreement. Enough to piss him off."

"Did you recognize the man she was with?"

"I didn't. I've never seen him riding here."

"When I come into the gate area and surrender my driver's license to Carlos, what does he do with it other than hold it until I leave?" said Cody.

Maya looked at him for a moment. "He copies all of them. Max asked him to maintain a record of every visitor, well, at least the drivers."

"So if he drove her the night of the party, we could find him even if she didn't care to tell us his name," I said. "I'm more interested in what we've learned about the nature of Raul's game. What can the old psychologist tell us?"

"That this is more about power than love, or even

sex. As you saw with Diana in a near comatose state, he owns them in every respect. He has stripped them of all their power. They cannot resist a single thing he does to them. He has shut down their humanity, their ability to act as a person. They cannot threaten him. Inside, Raul Sanchez was a little man."

"But where was *his* humanity" said Maya.

"Right. He has none either, even conscious and alert. Perhaps it's about reducing them to his level or below, so he can feel superior to them."

"Usually we look for this kind of behavior from the villain of the piece," I said. "Not the victim. How does he end up like this? You hate to blame the target, but he must have brought his death on himself."

Cody shrugged and took a slow sip of the Alma de Magno, a *solera* brandy. "Most of these behaviors originate in childhood. If Raul grew up with a monster parent, then he had no power from the beginning, and in his own defense, he would've learned to watch how power was acquired and applied. Later, once he got physically large enough, he must've started trying it out himself, first on his peers."

Maya put her hand on his shoulder. "So then he became the monster parent himself."

"And many of his women victims were as defenseless as children in his grip."

CHAPTER TWENTY

We decided that since I had already met Diana Freeman, I would be the one to approach her. Cody was a stranger and too far out of scale for her taut but delicate presentation, and as a fellow boarder, Maya didn't think Diana would open up as readily to her, since she would have to live with what she said when they saw each other nearly every day. I hadn't gotten far with Diana myself on the first meeting, when she seemed to be coming off a difficult riding session, and was not well composed. Now I had far more ammunition to work with.

I decided to meet her as if by accident in the parking corral. I knew approximately what time she finished in the ring, and I had come out with Maya the morning after our session with Raul's computer. I spent an hour and a half reading some horse magazines in the van, and then moved it into position at an angle about ten inches behind Diana's Mercedes coupe. In front of her car was a closely spaced row of eight-foot *organos* cactus, the kind with a single tall shaft that, when arranged in a row, screened the lot from the rest of the ranch. She couldn't get away except on foot.

Delgado called me as I sat there waiting. Nothing much was happening on the case, he said, although the police had rounded up three Central Americans on the quarry road near the Rancho Aria and, after questioning them, turned them over to the immigration authorities. Clearly he didn't have any more to offer.

He lingered on the line for a bit in case I did, but I wasn't ready to say anything about Raul's computer, which Cody was returning to his house at that moment. I was relieved that Delgado made no reference to the fiasco in Max's bedroom, and I was hoping he had by now reached the point where the information he'd gotten outweighed the embarrassment I had caused him. I think we both believed the next move (literally) would be up to Max himself. If discovering his mobility made him consider Max a suspect, Delgado didn't feel like offering that. This made me wonder what relations had been like between Max and Phaedra after we left that day. I'm sure the exchange was priceless.

As I hung up Diana came pacing briskly up the hill to the parking corral. She was swinging her arms as if in a good mood. That stopped when she saw how close my clunky but still newish van was parked next to her sleek little Mercedes sports car. I waved off her comment before she could make it.

"It's all right," I said, "you didn't do me any damage. It was kinda close, though." I felt like I had in Max's bedroom.

In the brilliance of the morning she had to shade her eyes to look up at me, since I had about ten inches of height on her. At that angle of full sun her indignation looked somewhat bleached out. Peering into her face that close I couldn't help but recall her unconscious features in those photos, and a strong surge of sympathy passed through me for what Raul had done to her. She must have seen it in my face. I almost put my hand on her shoulder, but that would not have been received in the way it was meant.

"I remember you. You're the one with Maya Sanchez." This after a quick glance to confirm nothing had violated her car's bumper. She reached over and rubbed it with two fingers and then studied them.

"Right. That Mexican woman again."

"Nothing happened here." She pointed at the space between the vehicles, her finger moving back and forth as if she had suddenly found a reason to be in a hurry.

"I know. I only wanted an excuse to talk to you."

"So talk. I know what you do for a living." Diana slipped into that posture I had noticed before; her hand extended palm upward with the elbow resting on her hip, and the other hip pushed out slightly.

"You had a good day today. Not every one goes that well."

"That's right, so don't spoil it for me."

"I'm looking into the death of Raul."

"Now you spoiled it."

"Imagine how he feels."

She straightened up and put both fists on her hips. "Today Raul is feeling the exact same thing he always felt—nothing. Death hasn't changed him one bit."

"I don't suppose anything *could've* changed him."

"That says it all, so why talk to me?" She pulled out her car key and clicked the door open. "If you wouldn't mind moving your van, I'd like to go home now."

I waited unmoving until she was about to step into the little coupe. "I have his photos of you."

Diana froze with one foot in and the other out, and looked up at me. "So I guess you're an underwear kind of guy, then. Good for you, but you would've seen more of me in a bikini, in case you've been thinking about it a lot."

"It goes way beyond that." I found myself liking her more, despite all the attitude she was giving me. She'd been through the Raul Sanchez sex mill and still kept her spirits intact.

"What do you want from me?"

"I'd like to take you off my list."

"Then take me off. I don't want to be on any guy's list who's twice as old as I am."

"I'm talking about suspects."

"I'm a suspect?"

"One of the best. Why don't you tell me about Raul."

With a long sigh Diana launched into what must have been the typical story. He had been hitting on her from the first week of her stint at Rancho Aria. At first she thought he was only being kind to single her out because she was new and a little tentative in a strange environment. Then he started touching her frequently, as if physically guiding her from place to place, gripping her elbow, then her hand.

"But you weren't new to riding. Didn't you have an experience before in Querétaro?" I chose the word *experience* for its vagueness.

Sitting on the edge of her car seat with her feet on the gravel, she unzipped her half chaps and pushed them behind her seat. I chose that moment to pull a hat out of my front seat.

"You sound like you think you might know something."

"I think I know a lot. Sometimes that's even true. Tell me why it isn't part of this situation."

"That boy in Querétaro was killed by the brother

of a girl he got pregnant. That's all I know. He was never charged."

"You weren't part of it."

"No, I hardy knew her very well, or him at all."

"What were your feelings towards Raul at the end? I know he was looking at your file a day or two before he died. I saw you gripping his arm at the boarder party. I noticed the expression on your face. That could only have been moments before he was killed. What were you looking for from him?" I handed her the photo I had printed out of her confronting him at the party. She glanced at it briefly and then ripped it in half, handing me back the pieces.

"I wanted him to destroy those photos. Instead you apparently inherited them, along with all the others, I'm sure. How many women were in those files? Thirty? Forty?"

I paused a moment for effect. "Four hundred and thirty-one." Placing her elbows on her knees, she leaned forward with her hands over her face. "Did you ever spend the night at his house?"

"No. He wanted me to. I mean, it was a fabulous place in a Mexican modern design sort of way, but even so, I always wanted to go home afterward. Sometimes I felt so tired I must have fallen asleep for a while because I remember waking up several of those times. It wasn't like it was that much of a workout—he was always done quickly."

"I think you were drugged. Could that have been?"

For the first time her expression suggested she thought I might be on her side. "Sometimes I was thirsty and my mouth felt very dry. I would drink a lot of water before I left."

"I'd like to hear a little more about his place. You said it was fabulous. Where was it?" Carlos' head bobbed out of the guardhouse, looking our way. I gave him a casual wave.

"It's a casita with a separate entrance a little way up Xichu, off Aldama, #6F. It's part of a larger property, but very private. You can't see into the main garden area, and no one can see you coming and going, unless they're standing on the street. That's what he liked about it."

"I'm sure. What ended it?"

"He did. He said he had what he needed from me and I was too young to keep up with him. I could've told him that myself."

"So then you killed him."

She shook her head slowly. "No, but I might've killed him for saying I was too old." She smiled.

"One more question. I'd like to talk to that man you were with at the party. I didn't recognize him from San Miguel, not that I know everyone in the expat community."

"I'm sure you didn't. He lives in Querétaro and he's my older brother, Don."

I gave Diana my card before I pulled the van clear of her car, and as if she were relieved, she waved warmly as she drove out. I had to wait for Maya to appear, and then we left too. The casita on Xichu explained a lot, starting with why Raul's house in Atotonilco was so nondescript, so uninviting to any woman not of his class and few who were. I began to imagine the kind of set up where he could entertain someone like Phaedra Montgomery, a woman whose name was still on my list. I still couldn't bring myself to think of her as Thelma Mae Perkins.

Was she part of the reason why Raul could afford such a place?

CHAPTER TWENTY-ONE

I filled Maya in as we drove home.

"I'm sure you did it better than I could've. I would have been too embarrassed to talk to her about her pictures. But do you think she's in the clear? Isn't that what you call it?"

"Who knows? I think she's too young to come off that genuine if she had anything to do with killing him. Anything about a new trainer?"

"No. Max has got Laszlo down in the paddock keeping order. He knows nothing about horses; he's only there to see that the grooms don't steal all the supplies. Half the riders have dug out their books and horsemanship magazines and are doing self-training."

Later I walked down to *centro* alone to pick up our mail at Caravan. At the edge of the *jardín* I ran into Amanda Klein. She looked like she was about to nod off on one of the cast iron benches. She brightened up on seeing me.

"I'll make it worth your while if you buy me a

cup of coffee."

I pulled her into a café under the arches. "I'm listening."

"There's been a change in the narrative," she said after we ordered.

"I had wondered if the book was still going forward, but I'm not surprised. You said there was something coming up, but you didn't know what. Perhaps Max foresaw this."

"I don't know how. Anyway, word has been put out that his miraculous cure came about from the application of a bottle of Lourdes water brought to him by a cousin just back from France."

"Really! Given his background I would've thought he'd been raised Southern Baptist rather than Catholic."

Amanda shrugged. "Well, either way it's all about the water and its uses, isn't it? It's always been a magical element in a lot of religions."

The waiter set two cappuccinos in front of us.

"Now that's the new tale you're going to write about. The story ends with a miracle, an element of hope for those unjustly oppressed by fate. Who can resist that kind of resolution? New York is going to love it. You've caught the formula."

"I know. Next you're going to tell me you believe that there's such a thing as nonfiction. Autobiography, for example."

"I hadn't thought about it, although we did talk about how you tweak the narrative now and then to have it make sense. Is this new wrinkle making sense?"

"Sometimes you have to settle for the fact that distantly plausible is as close as you're going to get. Remember, this book is his story, not mine." She blew on the cappuccino and took a careful sip, which left a white crescent of foam on her upper lip. "Now I have a question for you."

"Go ahead."

"What was your unofficial role in Max's 'cure'?"

I looked away. "You mean, did I bring the Lourdes water?"

"Don't balk at my question, because I feel like I sense your delicate touch in this. Like you painted the image of a hole on the floor and Max fell through it."

I showed her my poker face, although I couldn't help but think of all the information about Max she'd given me. "This is not for the record."

"Agreed."

I told her the story of our bedroom visit. We owed her at least that much.

"I wonder if you realize that Max has had two lengthy sessions of interrogation downtown with Licenciado Delgado because of this. Right over there." She pointed to the old Presidencia, where Delgado and several others from the Judicial Police had their office on the second floor, the same place where I had failed to get Maya and Cody released after sparring with Licenciado Según.

"I hadn't heard that Delgado had focused on him, but I'm not surprised. As Maya said after Max recovered his mobility, 'All the masks must come off,' and he had one of the more elaborate ones."

We fell silent as two ten-foot *mojigangas* passed by, the puppet figures with a human inside. Most of the rest of the crowd moving past were tourists.

"Some of the masks are going back on," Amanda said.

"What do you mean?"

"You have probably heard people say that many expats come down here and reinvent themselves, often whether they intend to or not."

"Sure, I've seen books written about it, although some of those folks don't want to think of it that way. They like to feel there's more continuity in the process. For them it's not a rebirth, only a new chapter."

"Now think of Max in that context. This is a rebirth for him, at least publicly. Going forward he has decided to be known as Alistair Kingman, dropping his first name. That's how it's going to appear now on the book."

For a moment I was speechless.

"I'm sure you noticed the paintings in the great room at the ranch house," she continued. "They were done as a family saga by an artist who was close to Max's great uncle, the man standing next to a fancy car with a horse."

"I heard about it. I thought the horse looked fancy too."

"That man was the original Alistair Kingman, and it was his passion for riding that began the family tradition that Max was injured trying to uphold. It began first in the East, and then continued when they came out to Texas around the time of the First World War."

"So Max is now his reincarnation."

"You could say that, and you were the midwife to that event, Paul Zacher. You are a man of many skills." Amanda patted the back of my hand, as if to say, Good job!

"My tools, such as they are, I keep at the ready. So Max seems to prefer any identity but his own real one. First he's the lifelong cripple, then he's his own great uncle. Will the real Max Kingman please stand up? I don't think he did the other day in his bedroom."

"But someone did. My task in this book is still to find out who that was."

We felt we were taking little risk as the three of us pulled up in front of Xichu 6F that afternoon. It was a low traffic area, and no one was outside on the steeply sloped street. Diana had been clear that once inside we would be invisible to anyone on the rest of the property. Maya and I stayed in the car while Cody worked on the lock without bothering to knock. No sense in all three of us going to jail if the cops went past, particularly with Maya's recent arrest history.

The façade told us nothing, but that was typical. The handsome, pale putty-green paint color was like that of my own house, a rare choice in a town dominated by reds, salmons, and yellows. The door was constructed of fashionably rusted steel, studded with three rows of tooled rosettes, and offering a small grilled view panel at face height. The hardware looked like the same sturdy quality. In slightly more than two minutes Cody swung open the door and walked inside. As we followed him I was still wondering where the money came from to support this stylish love nest for Raul Sanchez.

What I noticed first was that it all went together, a single unified concept. It was not my taste, but it was the taste of someone who had some. That meant Raul had collected the funds to spring for a decorator. The art, usually the first thing I look at, was all photography, some of it vintage shots of old San Miguel before any gringo had ever heard of it. Others were current street scenes in vivid color. I knew this was cheaper than paintings would've been. The furniture was clean in design and subdued in color with no acreage of masculine black leather, no exotic wood veneers, and no chrome. The flat screen television and a high tech sound system waited in a cabinet hand painted with Indian themes, but with an abstract character that made them look hip and current. The lighting was all chaste and unobtrusive.

At one end a kitchenette offered a premium coffee maker and a wet bar with microwave and a small fridge. At the opposite end a queen sized bed was dressed with white, almost virginal linens in a ribbed weave. At the door, a tall, narrow table finished in an eggplant lacquer offered a carved orange gourd bowl with a spray of business cards. They read, *décor by selena.*

In the small closet we discovered some clothing on hangers, and more to the point, at one side two tripods with a video and a still camera. We found no landline. The bathroom had premium fixtures from the States and luxurious Turkish towels. One wall was entirely mirrored.

What we searched for in vain was any trace of the real Raul Sanchez. Perhaps this was only the person he wished or pretended to be, an image he could buy and don like a costume, but from the meager storage and relative absence of clean clothing, changes of linen, and even many breakfast essentials and normal cooking utensils, he had rarely spent the night there. I wonder if he couldn't face his conquests in the

morning, or perhaps they couldn't face him, and preferred to wake up more securely alone and in their own
beds. He may have felt the need to return to his own
more modest digs in Atotonilco, where he could once
again be himself.

I was more and more getting the picture of a man
of low self-esteem, a man whose goal in his pursuit of
women was more about lowering them in his estimation
to enhance his own self-image than sexual enjoyment or
even power. In a way he was a bully who couldn't take on
other men, only women.

CHAPTER TWENTY-TWO
CODY WILLIAMS

Maya and Cody drove out to Rancho Aria later that day at a little before seven o'clock, quitting time for the paddock crew. They took Cody's small Ford to the entrance gate, less than four minutes from the edge of San Miguel. Maya provided the ticket inside. Although Carlos the gatekeeper recognized him now, Cody had no reason to be there without Maya, who told Carlos she had come to check on Martina, who had seemed to be favoring her left front hoof earlier that day.

On the way, she had given Cody a report on Rodrigo, the groom she had interacted with more than anyone on the staff, even Raul. The one most skilled and experienced with physically caring for the horses, he was burdened with a cyclical drinking problem, one that ramped up and made him undependable in appearing for work about every six weeks. He had the personality of a pressure cooker. Stewing during long periods of reliability, he would finally blow out and fail to reappear for four or five days running, often returning with a black eye and a missing tooth. He'd had two guns confiscated by the police. With one of them he'd landed in jail for shooting up something too public to be ignored in Colonia de la Paz, but no one was injured. In his day-to-day appearance in the paddock he was well regarded and appreciated by the riders.

"If he lives long enough, which I doubt," Maya said, "he will be a troublesome old man."

Planning for a casual interview, Cody had brought along a half-size bottle of white unaged tequila of the kind he thought Rodrigo probably favored.

When they reached the paddock without glancing up at the house, Maya broke off and went to Martina's stall while Cody caught up with Rodrigo as he was about to lock the tack room, newly fitted with a more secure closure.

"Let me buy you a drink," Cody said, after introducing himself as a person thinking about boarding there. "I need some information about how things work here now that Raul is gone. Someone told me it was a much different system."

Without comment Rodrigo went into the locked cabinet in the tack room next to the workbench that held equine medications and pulled out two plastic cups that looked fairly clean. They found a bench at the end of the stalls and sat down out of view of Max's loggia up the slope. In the long shadows, the groom's face was brown and deeply lined, although he was probably still in his early forties. His smile was cheerful, even missing three teeth. With his slight squint, Cody thought he looked like a bandito in a Hollywood B-grade western from the 1950s.

Wishing for a couple of ice cubes, Cody poured a round and touched his glass to Rodrigo's. "*Salud!* I suppose it's been tough without Raul around now." The tequila tasted like a concoction he'd add to the gas tank of an old car to make the engine run smoother. Cody preferred tall rum drinks with fruit juices and plenty of ice.

After a long sip, Rodrigo shrugged, not the most elaborate of Mexican shrugs, but a lesser version, as if the issue were not doubtful enough to merit the full production on short notice. "We will be OK like this for a while, I think. Raul was not the only one to know the horses. I am with them every day. Raul was more about the boarders."

"Is anyone coming in to replace him? I don't suppose you've heard anything."

"But, yes, we have heard some talk about a trainer from outside of Monterrey, name of Braganza. A big name, I suppose, up there. He is from a more important rancho and wishes to have less responsibility now, as he is only five years from retirement."

"What do you think of that?"

Rodrigo gave him a careful look, peering over the edge of his plastic glass. "You are with Señorita San-chez?"

Cody gave him a broad smile. "Yes, I am her uncle from Chicago, by marriage, of course. The whole family is very proud of her."

"Well, I think Señor Braganza is looking for a rancho that mainly serves the gringos, you know? To get away from certain things on the border, this is what people are saying around here. I don't know for certain. They don't tell me everything."

"But what if Max would not be paying him as much as he would get on a bigger rancho?"

"It could be. But there are always more ways to make money for the trainer, since he controls so many things."

"Ah! I hadn't thought of that." Cody had thought of nothing else since he'd seen Raul's love nest. "I sup-pose he must give extra riding lessons."

Erupting in laughter, Rodrigo covered his mouth and handed his empty glass back to Cody with the other hand. "You have some things to learn about this place, I think."

Overhead a layer of late summer clouds was collecting. Along the adjacent row of stalls and the one opposite, the horses were settling in for the evening, sheltered against the thickening weather. As lights came on around the paddock, some called out to each other. A thin rumble of thunder rolled by, but it came from far away, closer to Dolores Hidalgo on the road going north. Up at Casa Kingman two lanterns on the porch went on, but the loggia on the closer end of the house remained unlit. Cody wondered if Max might be up there watching, unobserved.

"Why do I think you could be my teacher, Rodrigo? Am I right? Talk to people on the ground, I always say, the same people who are there every day to see what happens with the animals."

"Well, I will start with the matter of selling the manure. Thank you for this." He raised his refilled glass.

Like that's a big money maker, Cody thought. What was horse manure bringing these days on the open market? Was he wasting his time on Rodrigo?

"Once every week the brick makers from Pantoja come to buy the manure, which we pile up behind these stalls. You cannot see it from the paddock. That's where the chickens are too, picking at the flies. Señor Max hates the flies."

"The brick makers are buying it?"

"Yes, since they mix it with the clay for bricks to build houses. Then they bake them."

"OK. What is wrong with that?"

"It is the tradition here and in other ranchos that the money from the manure is divided among the grooms. When Raul came here he stopped that and kept it all for himself. It set a bad tone at the beginning, as you can see."

"That can't be so much money, though, is it?"

"Not by itself. But there are other things the trainer has always had for his own."

Cody nodded as he took a minuscule sip from his glass. He felt that, had there been a candle lit between them, his breath could've flared up as it passed over the flame.

"Fringe benefits, I suppose."

Rodrigo gave him a curious look. "Hay would be one. When the farmer comes with a load of hay he puts it in the barn. Let us say there are 300 bales. Then Raul goes up to the house and says we have received 350 bales. Max gives him the money for that many and Raul pays the farmer for 300."

"And there is no paperwork to get in the way of this?"

"You know how things go here. No paper, and everything is done in cash to avoid the tax."

"What else?"

"The same thing happens again with the farrier. Say twelve horses are shod and then Raul collects for fourteen from Max and pays for twelve. And the vet is the same. So you see now how it goes."

"And he had to keep the manure money on top of this."

"That's the way he was. He had to have everything for himself."

"Everything but the loyalty of the grooms." Cody stood up and looked over the paddock where the shadows were deepening. The horses were murmuring as they settled down. He poured Rodrigo another drop or two and slid the bottle toward his side of the small table. "And the next question I want to ask is why Raul had to have all the women too."

Rodrigo nodded slowly. "That is why Pilar Ruiz said she would have to kill him."

CHAPTER TWENTY-THREE

Cody phoned that evening suggesting it was time for me to pay a call on Pilar. He made the case in two sentences why I should be the designated interviewer again. I didn't mind, since Drake had piqued my curiosity about her. I had gotten the impression at the party of a woman with a powerful emotional makeup, although her distress at Raul's murder seemed to contradict the idea that she had killed him.

Cody and Maya had paused on the way out of Rancho Aria and picked up her new address from Carlos the gatekeeper. Now they were on their way back. He didn't know Pilar, Cody said, although he had heard the story of her and Drake from us. It looked like my kind of job, and Maya agreed.

I thought about it for a while. My first instinct was to approach her through Drake Wilson, but I didn't have a sense of where they were in their relationship at that time, and I didn't want to ask him. I also didn't want him to screen her from my questions, or warn her that I was coming, and it was more than likely he had never heard her threat against Raul, which may even have come before Drake started boarding at Rancho Aria. Cody was already regretting that he had forgotten to ask Rodrigo when that threat was made.

It looked like we were moving closer to the endgame on this case, one where no one had ever hired us and no one was likely to pay us. I was starting to feel like a not very bright super hero without a cape. What kept us going with it was that if we solved it, the crime would never come back to haunt Maya. That was payment enough.

Pilar Ruiz lived in a newer part of the La Lejona neighborhood, almost at the edge of the all white El Secreto development. It's in the southeast corner of town, tucked behind the Mega supermarket. The street whose name Carlos the gatekeeper had given Maya and Cody had been built up within the last three or four years.

It was a still, chilly morning when I pulled up in front of a pale yellow house. The entry and the garage door were both painted a coppery brown in the style I call Mexican Modern. The look is about massing and shape, all cubes and rectangles, and no detail or trim is used. To my taste it feels theoretical and abstract. The windows often do not open enough to admit the wonderful fresh air of a spring day. Although my head hosts a ton of them, I don't want to live inside an idea; I want a functioning house with some esthetic values. The neo-colonial style in San Miguel, with its arches, paned windows, and stone trim, its sunny gardens and shady alcoves, is usually preferred by expats for that reason. Mexicans are less sentimental about their colonial past, perhaps because it contains so many bad memories.

The rectangular ceramic plaque set into the stucco next to the bell read la Familia Arroyo. That must be Pilar's sister and her husband.

I rang the bell and mounted a welcoming look on my face, although I had no idea what to expect of Pilar, or if she was even at home. My recollection of her at the party suggested that, while she had a lively manner, she might also be a little ragged emotionally, and Drake's story supported that. A few seconds later the tiny door on a small grilled opening swung inward and displayed part of her face, enough to show me how surprised she was. There may have been a subtle flash of fear in her dark brown eyes too. Not the reaction I wished to inspire.

"I remember you from the party. You looked at me so hard I had to turn my face away. Drake told me you are a detective."

"I'm sorry, but that's how I see people. I'm Paul Zacher and I need to talk to you about that party. Can I come in?" With what Drake had told me about her blow up that evening after they left for home, I didn't want to say Raul's name, at least not to start.

She nodded slowly. The small viewing door closed and the larger one opened. I walked into a narrow airspace fronting the house, about two meters deep, one that provided light to a series of windows along the front. Pilar led me into a living room dining room combination. Some of the furniture was nearly new, upholstered in a magenta plush fabric and edged in dark polished wood. If it made a statement it was not about comfort, it was more about having one formal and extravagant new thing to go with the new house. The dining table was well worn, with eight chairs that came from two different sets. The walls offered a couple of religious prints, and the other furniture clustered around a flat screen television. This house looked like a stretch for the Arroyos.

Pilar invited me to take a seat at a small breakfast table overlooking a garden in the back. No one else was present. "Coffee? I have some made."

"OK."

Pilar wanted to speak in English, saying as she poured me a cup that she'd gone to high school and part of middle school in San Diego. For college she had come back to México and attended one year in Guanajuato. Then she ran out of money.

At the party, the closest I'd come to her was seeing her from across the room, but I recall thinking she was quite attractive. With large liquid eyes and a tall, trim build, she might have been five-foot-eight. That morning she was wearing a well-worn dress cut on the bias, so that the mauve and gray woven fabric had a way of clinging to her figure as she moved. With a large, expressive mouth, her face seemed to reflect all her emotions as soon as she felt them. As at the party, a comb on each side kept her hair off her face, and it fell in coarse waves down her back.

"I'm working with the police on the murder." I didn't know whether this would set her off again, but there was no more subtle way to say it.

Pilar only nodded. She folded her hands on the enameled steel table as we sat on folding chairs. From somewhere nearby, in a back yard or patio one or two houses down, a small dog began to yap insistently, as if imprisoned in a dungeon, and our voices had reached it.

"He always barks like that when no one is home over there."

"How often is that?"

"Every day." She shrugged.

"I wonder if you could describe how Raul looked, what his manner was like and what he was doing the last time you saw him at the party."

Her eyes immediately welled up, and she turned away to look into the garden, a rectangular raised bed framed in smooth concrete with pavers around it. It did not invite anyone to come out and sit there, even if there had been any shaded seating. It looked more like a grave waiting for a headstone.

"Raul was very angry."

"Who was he talking to?"

Pilar thought for a moment. "He had been talking to Diana for a while, not long, and she was trying to persuade him of something, I don't know what. Drake was pulling me away, pulling and pulling. Finally we went out to the porch. I didn't see Raul again after he went into the kitchen."

"No one followed him in from the party?"

"If anyone did I didn't see it. Perhaps after we went outside." Her hands worked at each other as they lay on the table, the fingers twisting together. They were more revealing than she was.

"This is hard, isn't it?" As I leaned back in my chair the dog yapped louder.

Pilar nodded and looked over my shoulder, not at my face. Her features wilted and her mouth opened wider in pain, but she added nothing. She looked like she was about to burst into tears or start screaming. Perhaps both.

"Were you a rider at Aria?" This was a more neutral subject that might keep her from breaking down.

She sighed as if looking back on a better time. "Only a little, now and then, and long ago. I couldn't afford a horse. Raul would get me mounted sometimes, without paying. Later I rode Buck too, when Drake first came to board. I don't think Max minded. It was like giving Raul, and then Drake, a perk. He knew I didn't have any money."

"Did you get along well with Raul?"

Pilar looked at me with alarm, almost with terror. The palm of her right hand began lightly rubbing the surface of the table for no clear reason. She rose abruptly and her skirt whirled around as she faced the garden window with her arms folded. Something in the way her dress clung to her, draped her body as she moved, began to fascinate me. It looked like it had once been a party dress for the cooler season, or a going out to lunch kind of dress that had been washed too many times but was still too good to throw away. The neckline and sleeves showed a couple of small wear points on the edges. As completely inappropriate as it seemed, in seeing that dress I could feel how deeply sensuous she was. In my mind I slammed the door on that train of thought.

"If you don't want to answer that," I said, "you don't have to. I'm just trying to understand some of the relationships at Rancho Aria, and it seems like a very complicated place." I had no reason or desire to be unprofessional with her. That was never my style. I studied her face as she sat down again, unable to avoid noticing the way the fabric modeled her breasts as she settled in and adjusted her skirt. She covered her twisted face with both hands.

I finished my coffee, now nearly cold, and waited for her to come around as I slid the cup to the side, where the salt and pepper shakers waited with a half-full bottle of Serafina Black Label hot sauce. It was the kind I preferred. She reached out and squeezed my hand, patted it briefly, then pulled back as if she hadn't meant to do that, an impulse she shouldn't have trusted.

"Thank you. You're very kind." Her mouth remained slightly open for a moment, but she didn't look at me. "But I will answer your question." She pulled her chin up.

I gave her an encouraging smile.

"Well, I was with Raul Sanchez for almost two years. As I think about it now, I can't tell you why."

"I'm sure you thought he was something special. He was an important trainer."

An ironic grin crossed her features and she set her chin on her palm, elbow on the table, and looked out onto the unappetizing garden. "Did you ever make a serious mistake in a relationship? Did you ever pick the wrong person or keep it going for too long when it wasn't working? Did you ever ask yourself how you got tangled up in something that wasn't any good for you, that hadn't ever been good for you?"

"Yes." I didn't want to go into detail for a variety of reasons. The main one was that I wasn't the person who had threatened to murder Raul, but several others also came to mind.

Pilar studied my clouded face for a moment. "But worst of all, have you ever been alone; really, deeply, alone?"

As she said it, the word seemed to echo with significance before she rushed on.

"I've been alone for ten days now, ever since the night of the party. You can't imagine what it's like to lose everyone at once like that. I can't bear to be alone, I never could. I don't know how it happens to me so often."

"I'm sorry," I said. She means losing both Raul and Drake the same night, I thought. Shaking her head, and without answering, she rose and carried the coffee cups to the sink counter, as if that new idea would take me a while to digest. From the back, the drape of her skirt was enticing as she moved; her walk was like a subtle dance.

"I feel like I know you now, I feel like I can really *trust* you," she said, without turning around. "Do you know how rare that is?"

"What?" This took me off guard. "But don't trust me so quickly, OK? I'm just a detective here. My only loyalty is to this case." I didn't feel like mentioning justice; the two ideas didn't always fit together, or even go in the same direction.

Pilar turned to face me. "Even so, Paul. I feel so close to you now, just talking like this. It's as if you've

JOHN SCHERBER

released me from the prison of my thoughts, and I don't know how you could this soon. I can't even talk like this to my sister, and we were always like that." She wrapped two of her fingers around each other. "What I feel now is like an instinct, or an intuition, about you." Here she launched the full-blown Mexican shrug and turned back to the sink.

"I'm glad you're feeling more comfortable," I said neutrally.

"Some things are just like that, I mean, when you really *know* something. I should've left Drake a long time ago, but I didn't feel like I could. He was boring, OK? That relationship was never any more than comfortable, but I knew that if I stayed with him I would have nice clothes and I would never be hungry again. That doesn't make me sound like a very good person, does it? But it's true."

Wiping her hands, she came around behind me and put them both on my shoulders, softly working the muscles through my shirt. "You probably already knew that about me, you're such a good detective." She bent over and nuzzled my neck like it was the most natural thing in the world to do. Two doors down, the yapping dog paused for a moment, as if in utter surprise. A current ran through Pilar's fingertips, through her lips as they seared my skin, and my short hairs stood on end. After enjoying this too much for about ten seconds, I searched for a way to stop it without physically shoving her away.

"Is this how it started with Raul, too?" She yanked her hands and face away, leaping back, or perhaps even ducking, as the question sailed over her head. She made no move to respond to it. An amused look slowly came over her face.

"Oh, you're quite the spoiler, Paul Zacher, I can see that now, and I like that so much about you! You are not that *easy*, and neither am I, so we're going to be such a good match, challenging each other just like we are today!"

I began to feel I had missed a critical transition or two. Were we now on our third date? She took a forthright step closer with her breasts thrust toward me, and tilted her head. Her voice took on a softer note. "Have you ever paused for a moment in your busy investigations to think about *destiny*?" One eyebrow went up as she placed her index finger fondly on her cheek, creating a dimple that did not at all damage her presentation. The way she pronounced the word *destiny* sounded like it could be an inspirational part of a theme park in northern Florida, along with rides devoted to Chip and Dale, Snow White, and especially to Goofy, the role I now found myself playing with far too little preparation, based on a script improvised by someone else. By this point I was only trying to keep up with her, although I was already sensing that was a doubtful bet.

"I despise the idea of destiny." Scrambling for dignity more than truth, I realized I had put both hands in my pockets, as if to protect them, or more probably, to keep them from sliding up her thighs. As she moved around the kitchen, her prancing, half-covered legs with their perfect skin were more enticing than any logic now on the table, not that there was any.

"So do I! I hate destiny too! Who knew we were so much alike?"

"I suppose it was never destiny when you were with Drake?"

"Past tense is correct. I thought at the time he was saving me from what was going on with Raul, but he's such a wimp! Always trying to act so nice, as if he really was. Anyway, I could never teach him about real passion. He didn't get it."

"Now I'm starting to think you know something about passion, perhaps more than most people."

Pilar put both hands on her hips and swirled her skirt as she leaned toward me.

"Yes, I do!"

"And did Raul know something about it too? Did he teach you, or was it the other way around?"

A quiet, level space opened up in this conversation, as if bridging two incompatible worlds. Her mouth closed and she stared at me with less expression than before. It was almost a softer kind of sadness, and something else, as if a new element was working behind her eyes. For the first time, Pilar Ruiz appeared slightly veiled. I wouldn't have thought her capable of it. The silence stretched into discomfort as we both waited for one of us to make the next move. I took the cue because I was afraid of what hers might be.

"I saw the photo of you that Raul sent Drake. The one where you were bent over with your hands tied behind you."

Her steady look held mine. "He made me feel like a child again, a very bad child that needed punishing. It was exciting. I had forgotten all about that." A fierce light flared up in her eyes, like a door opening in a furnace. In trying to restart the conversation I must have said the wrong thing. Pilar took a long step forward and pulled me out of the chair by my wrists. I hadn't imagined she was so strong. She gripped my right leg between both of hers, and her pubic bone bit into my thigh like a hungry animal. As my arms went around her on their own impulse, I felt like she was surging against me naked.

"We could be together like that, too!" Her voice was hoarse as if it came from a different part of her body, or mind.

"I'm not the one for you," I said, shaking my head against her cheek. "Really, Pilar, I have someone already. I have a life that I love and someone to share it with. I know you're hurting, but this is not the remedy. Anyway, you don't even know me. I have to go now." Feeling the desperation welling out of her, I pressed her head into my shoulder to give her a moment of comfort. She began kissing my neck as if I had said nothing.

Something tore as I gripped her shoulders to push her away. She held onto me, and the hot sauce bottle pitched over as I shook her off, spattering the table as the cap came free and rolled away over the edge. Her foot caught on the table leg and she sat down hard on the floor and then leaped at my ankle. Tripping over my chair, I scrambled for the door. As I reached the sidewalk, fumbling with my keys, Pilar seized my belt from behind. I lunged at the handle of my car door, just catching it.

"Wait, Paul, you don't understand. We're perfect for each other! You're thinking that I'm needy but I'm not. Just give me a chance. Your girlfriend doesn't have to know!" Her eyes were wild. A seam had ripped open at the top of her sleeve to expose a crescent of shoulder skin.

I was partly inside of my van and straining to close the door as she struggled to pull it toward her when the garage doors opened beyond us just a few feet away and a station wagon pulled up on the sidewalk. Inside, a woman stared at us with her mouth hanging open in disbelief, as two children about six and eight pressed their faces and palms against the rear window in dismay, screaming, "Tia Pilar! Tia Pilar!"

Pilar stopped in alarm and released her grip on the door handle. I nearly yanked it closed on my ankle. In that instant of distraction, I slammed the driver door shut at last. As I raced away from the curb I heard the yapping dog whipped into a psychotic frenzy.

I had made it as far as the Celaya highway and all the way down to the *glorieta* at the Mega supermarket before my pulse stopped surging. "Don't ever forget that I am a seasoned investigator," I muttered to a garbage truck in the next lane as we both wheeled around the circle.

I hadn't gotten to several of my prepared questions in this exchange, and I had thought of several more as I rushed away. Why had she threatened to kill Raul, for example? This was the reason I'd come out to talk to her to begin with. When did she say that, and why had she started seeing him again just before the party? Who was in control in that relationship and who had dumped who in the past? Worse, who was in control in this investigation? If this was the way Pilar was wired, how could she have chosen Drake Wilson, who was, in my view, just as staid and bombproof as his sexless horse, Buck? He displayed the passion of a mushroom, living as if he never left the shade.

In my hurry to get away from Pilar Ruiz, who had certainly gotten me going, I confess that I still left feeling more shaken than stirred. I do appreciate women who frankly enjoy sex, but this was far from my idea of foreplay. I wondered if every new relationship was an instant source of pain for her even as it appeared to be a flash of enlightenment. Did they all start with this degree of intensity? I tried to imagine Drake in my place in that kitchen and came up with nothing. Was this the new courtship? After nearly ten years with Maya, perhaps I was out of touch.

My final unanswered question was how Pilar could simply stand at the sink wearing an old worn dress, rinsing two coffee cups and still generate such an erotic current? Like a field of attraction, you could not step into it without being polarized by its effect. I couldn't even think how to paint this phenomenon, since it had no visual component. It might as well be an edgy taste under your tongue.

After that encounter I didn't feel like I could face Maya, or anyone else, for a while, so I parked the van down on Canal below the overpass and walked back up to the *jardín*. There I had a chocolate ice cream from the horse wagon while I sat on a cast iron bench and watched the blur of the passing crowd, seeing not a single person individually. In my mind I was replaying line by line that tragic farce I had just emerged from, and it wasn't coming out any better than it did the first time. Destiny was not a word I planned to use again for a long time.

After a time I began to realize that this had not been about me, and it was not even about Drake Wilson. I was only someone to reach for in a tough moment. This was still about Raul Sanchez. I saw Pilar as one of the 431 women on Raul's list. Was his specialty the needy, the lonely, the women trapped in a relationship without passion or life? Had this been his appeal to Phaedra, who seemed to have nearly everything else? My own sense of Raul matched Cody's. He was a small man who needed to reduce other people to his own scale. He found it easier to do this with women than with men. If Pilar had found passion with him, it was within herself. When Drake had turned out to be a long-term bore, she had gone back to relight that spark with Raul. To him it must have been no more than a second round of triumph.

This all made me wonder whether Pilar Ruiz was both predator and prey.

CHAPTER TWENTY-FOUR

It often happens that the Zacher Agency reaches a certain point in an investigation where it slows to a halt as if we've hit a speed bump too high to clear. That's the way I felt that day after I returned from the *jardín*. At lunch I didn't tell Maya much about the Pilar meeting, other than that I'd come up with nothing helpful to the case. I described her as being in an emotionally unstable condition, which was no surprise, and mentioned that I was still sorting through the conversation myself, looking for usable information. I didn't add that I saw no sign that Pilar would have caused Raul's death except by wearing him out sexually, and that wouldn't have happened on the unyielding tiles of the storage room floor.

The case still hinged on who had followed Raul into the kitchen. As much as I didn't like the idea, it was time to probe Delgado and see whether he would share anything with us. My instinct was always to save these rescue calls for a real emergency, which this was not. His people had interviewed the entire party crowd, and while I had heard his money was still on Max as the killer, it might be that he'd found a witness or two who could place someone else in the kitchen at the right time.

Once I reached him at the office we went through the usual courtesies. His older son was about to start his second year in law school in Guanajuato, and the other boy was also doing well.

"How is your investigation going?" I said, after he told me his health was also holding up well. He added that he had not finished the rest of the Herradura Añejo we gave him, saving it for the resolution of the case.

"Anyway, the case is still going, but not very fast. We are still thinking that Señor Kingman is our man."

"He hasn't confessed?"

"No, but we have another conversation scheduled for this afternoon during *comida*. It is a war of nerves. When he becomes indignant from my questions I remind him of how he lied to everyone for more than forty years."

"Still, I wonder what his motive would be?"

"Revenge, since we feel there was a sexual connection with Señora Montgomery."

"Has she acknowledged that?"

"No, and she no longer speaks to us."

"I've been thinking that someone else might have been seen entering the kitchen after Raul Sanchez. I know you have spoken to everyone who attended the party."

"Yes."

While helpful, this was an answer that offered substantially less detail than I was looking for. I sensed some reluctance on his part to address the question.

"Do you have a witness?"

"Well, yes. We have found three, to be truthful."

"I expected nothing less. Was it Max they observed?"

"No."

"I see. That's good, right? So you have at least one more suspect, should Max turn out to be the wrong man."

"Perhaps, but we have decided not to go forward from this information."

I could make out a soft regular tapping on his end, as if he were impatiently drumming a pencil eraser on his desktop.

Once again, here was a possible parallel to situations we had seen before, a suspect with enough immunity to avoid police interrogation. Everything is about connections here, and this was not the first time we'd seen them interfere with an investigation. I tried to think who at the party might be set up with that degree of clout, since in all probability Delgado would not even tell me who the person was, although I felt I had to ask.

"Here in the Zacher Agency we are still searching

for other possible killers, since we know how thorough you are being with Max Kingman. Can I have the name of this new suspect so we can look at that person while your forces are so focused elsewhere?"

"Well, if you wish, although there could be some awkwardness about it."

"I can handle it." Get on with it, I thought. I don't have enough going on with this case to be pussyfooting around anymore.

"The person the three witnesses saw enter the kitchen after Raul was you, Señor Zacher. No one else went in until Señor Cody Williams arrived."

Listening to him chuckle, I signed off after thanking Delgado for not arresting me. But this information was still worth something, because it suggested that the killer must have come in through the back door of the storeroom. This had always been a possibility, and for Delgado I'm sure it must've reinforced the idea of Max as the perpetrator.

After lunch I called Cody and invited him to join us in a trip out to Rancho Aria. It would be a final walk through in hopes of turning up something we had missed. None of us was feeling hopeful, but neither did we have any other ideas. Since it was a Thursday, Maya had not been there that morning to ride.

"I still think Delgado's off base about Max," said Cody as we passed the bus station on the way to the

Libramiento overpass. "He had too much to lose by the trainer's death, and frankly, I think he's too disengaged from Phaedra to care who she's going to bed with. That's just my take on it. Remember her reaction when he jumped up out of his chair. That was not the comment of a supportive person. When we talked to him earlier, he also wasn't surprised that Raul had been killed, and if he had done it himself, in my experience, he would've acted like he was."

"And after talking to her you still think it was not Pilar," Maya said to me from the back seat. Cody always needed the longer legroom in front.

I told them a bit more about my conversation with her, about the emotional tightrope she walked and how she tended to invest in people too quickly with little reason beyond her own immediate needs. I framed all this as coming from my observations, not based on her approach. "Since she placed a huge emphasis on how alone she was after Raul's death, I don't see her killing him. And while she certainly has some characteristics of the victim, I also saw elements of the predator in her. An emotional predator."

"And you believed that," Maya said. Her tone offered no comment on whether I should have or not.

"In that context, I did. I don't think she has the control or the discipline to be a good liar. Everything she says seems to come right off the top of her head."

"Then maybe she's the best," said Cody. "What better cover for a liar than to seem incapable of lying?"

I didn't respond to that. You have to go with your gut feeling.

"You seem more rational about her now," said Maya, primly.

I looked at her over my shoulder. "You're right. I didn't know how to handle Pilar. She made me wonder who Drake Wilson really is. What do we think about Phaedra herself?" I wasn't sorry to move on.

"I think the ice pick method is too physical for her," said Maya. "She pretends to be very classy and wellborn, and that kind of personal violence is not a good fit. It may match what she feels in her true self, but she never falls out of character, at least that I've seen. I'd give her more thought if Raul had been poisoned."

"But to go back a few steps, what about Drake Wilson?" Cody said. "We know Pilar had started seeing Raul again right before the party. Drake was most anxious to make his disclosure to you, Paul, when doing that made him look forthright and open, even though the facts of it gave him a reason to take his revenge on Raul. Stepping forward like you have nothing to hide is often an effective cover for a faulty position. Right away he comes running over to tell you something you're likely to discover on your own, that he has a good motive. By doing that he gains credibility and loses nothing."

"And by saying it himself," added Maya, "he can put his own spin on it, instead of having you hear it from someone else phrased in a way he can't control."

"Could be," I said, "although I sense that he's too stoic, too calm to commit a murder. Killing Raul was a spur of the moment crime with a weapon ready to hand and in a location that could not have been planned. I don't see Drake as that spontaneous or passionate, nor is he bright enough to figure out how to use that confession to me as a strategy to cover his guilt."

"I don't know," Cody said, "Still waters and all that. He might be hiding an explosive temper gene somewhere, and one for deviousness as well."

"What about the train wreck people?" said Maya. "They're still out there, some of them, anyway. I haven't gone on any trail rides since the wreck. But if the murderer came in through the back door of the storage room…"

"And they're the wild card," I said. "You can't find any of them to talk to, so you can't assess what their condition is, their state of mind. How many of them were criminals back home, if any, we can't ever find out. The fact that they steal things here tells us nothing except that they're desperate. I guess Raul might have caught one in the storeroom, but were they likely to try to come into the house that night with all that party activity going on? I don't see it."

"Someone else, then," said Maya. "That writer? Amanda Klein? You talked to her a lot."

I only shook my head as we drove up to the gate. I couldn't see her in this. "I think she's mainly engaged by her book, and she doesn't connect much with anything outside of that process. I haven't seen her interacting with anyone else other than Max and me, even at the party."

Carlos was munching as he let us through the gate. It was a few minutes after two, when the Mexican workers' lunch begins. I felt like this was our last shot, even as I couldn't see what more we might turn up in this visit.

"Look at *everything*," was Cody's last comment as he went down the path to the paddock in search of Rodrigo. Cody had thought of a couple more questions fro the groom about Pilar's startling threat. As far as I was concerned, if he came up with more questions for her he could go ask them himself.

"We're not going to get into the house," Maya said, "at least not through the front door."

"Then let's try the loading area in the back and the storage entrance." On foot we followed the service road from the parking corral to the side of the house away from the terrace, seeing no one around. Four or five expansive old mesquite trees screened the loading area, and no truck was present. The rear door of the storage room stood open, but the only person present was Ivan, the mentally challenged son of the cook, Ofelia. I had noticed him on one of my early visits working with a yard crew, where his principal task appeared to be holding a waste bag so someone else could fill it, but I'd never had a close look at him.

It was a quiet shady place with only a small disturbance going on in the trees as the birds sorted out the ownership of some tidbit. This space so close to the kitchen had to provide good scavenging. Ivan's back was toward us as he bent over the table working on something I couldn't see. An empty plate and a soda can were near his elbow. Any household staff person in town would've loved to have a place like this to eat or take a break. Extra space there was at a premium.

Maya crossed to the storage room door as I walked over to the plank table where Ivan sat.

"*Buenos días.* What are you working on today?" I asked.

Ivan grinned with pride as he set down his pocketknife and handed me an ice pick. His ingrained sense of class differences made him reluctant to look directly at me. He was chipping the handle out from a block of soft wood about an inch square and five inches long. It was now mostly roughed in with the shape of a coarse grip, just like the one on the pick that had killed Raul. It had been drilled vertically, and the tang of an old rat tail file, where the business part was round in section, had been tapped into it. A grinding wheel had roughly smoothed the teeth off it. At the tip it was ground to a lethal point.

I had never seen the blade of the tool that killed Raul, but for a scant inch between the handle and the skin of his neck, but it must have been like this one, about an eighth of an inch in diameter. Worn out files were common and easy to find around the paddock where metalwork on fencing and horseshoes went on regularly at a small bench at the back of the tack room.

"Very nice job," I said, sitting down next to him. "I guess you must have lost your other one somewhere." I handed it back to him. "It was probably one of the tools used to carve the horse's head in that block of ice, right?"

I was just starting to wonder if Ivan might be mute when he nodded and looked at me for the first time. I blinked, stunned to see that his eyes were the same vivid blue as those of Max Kingman, and also those of Max's great uncle, Alistair, in the Leyendecker painting. A sudden icy insight came over me.

"I hope your mother is all right now," I said slowly, scanning his face. "Did Raul hurt her badly?"

"He kicked her. Kicked her hard." Ivan was nodding as he spit this out. "Said I shouldn't be in there eating. It was a party for big people. Only them."

"Did you tell your dad what happened then?"

He shook his head vigorously. "Never tell dad.

Mother said that. Never tell dad because they're not married anymore. Never tell him anything. Now he can walk."

"Is Max a good dad for you?"

He looked at me as if this were an idea he'd never considered.

"Never see him." He shrugged.

From behind me I heard a muted yelp. I spun around to see Ofelia's stout form charging out of the storage room behind Maya, shooing her out with both hands, and at that instant she must've caught sight of me talking to Ivan. She turned and started to scream, "Get away, boy, run away! Don't talk to him! He'll hurt us!"

I turned back and rested my right hand on his wrist to reassure him, my other palm still flat on the table, but Ivan whirled and the flash of the ice pick came slicing down toward my hand. I started to jump up, but before I could get away, the blade bit deeply into the surface between my outspread fingers. Ivan struggled to withdraw it but it didn't come out. With a moan he turned and ran. At that moment Cody strode through the gap in the trees with a long step, wearing a frustrated look. Maya screamed, "Hold him!"

Cody caught Ivan in a bear hug, then twisted his arm behind him until he relaxed and hung his head.

CONCLUSION

No one thought it unusual that for Diego Delgado, the end to the case came as a back room deal with the Kingman family. Ivan was committed to a private secure mental facility in León. Delgado told us that such mentally challenged people often ended up in the general prison population when they committed violent crimes. Max was able to prevent this. This refuge was based in an old aristocratic townhouse with a broad garden in the center. From the photos I saw, it was physically a better place to live than Maya and I had on Quebrada. Their website spoke of all the crafts they offered to occupy their wards. Ivan would find a way to keep busy.

In a strange way, our killer looked like nearly the only innocent player in the whole story. He had no evil or deceit in him. Max, or as he was now known, Alistair Kingman, (we in the Agency had begun to call him New Alistair, somewhat like New Brunswick), would foot the bill for Ivan's care and make provision in his will for the time when he was gone. It was Laszlo who found Ofelia a place to rent quite near to Ivan's new digs, since Alistair never left the rancho anymore, possibly fearing questions he didn't care to answer. She was pensioned off and no murder charge was ever filed against Ivan. I tried without success to imagine the farewell between father and son, since Ivan's name had never come up. In his marriage to the young and willowy Ofelia, had Max's bloodlines fallen short of the Kingman standard? Perhaps this had been seen as yet another unspoken failure of his undisciplined youth, and worse, another one of those consequences the family could not repair. Max and Phaedra had remained childless, just as Max was not ready to ever jump again.

Cody and Maya both professed to be comfortable with that resolution. Ivan was a man of diminished capacity, and his crime was a spur of the moment event in defense, as he perceived it, of his mother. None of us believed that Raul, in a fit of anger after his bitter scolding by Diana Freeman, meant to do any more than kick Ofelia. She was only the next female victim in his path, one of no special significance, but you couldn't say what Ivan was thinking at that moment. He may have seen my presence next to him at the table on that last day as just one more threat to her by yet another person with more status than he had, a group that included everyone at Rancho

Aria down to the lowest groom who mucked out the stalls.

I couldn't help regard Raul's assault on Ofelia, while not sexual, as still one more token of his overall abuse of women. He had died for his attitudes and practices, and it did not escape us in the Agency that no staff person or owner at Aria, no boarder, and no one of the five investigators involved had ever shed a single tear for his demise. The unspoken conclusion was that Raul had gotten what he deserved.

As for what Raul's family made of this, we never heard. It's possible that he may not have been popular among his relatives. Sexual abuse among families occurs here as elsewhere, and this settlement may have been perceived as appropriate. They got to unload and carry off the contents of both his lodgings, and sell off his pickup. More than this, perhaps none of Raul's family wanted to second guess the justice system and confront the financial might of the Kingmans.

There was no way to announce it subtly, but Cody had by this time erased all the photos and records dealing with Raul's amorous escapades, his "entertainments," and replaced the wiped down laptop in that small desk in his house. I had already done the same with the copy I had made on my own computer.

At the end, I was not surprised that Maya was unable to reestablish her comfort zone at Rancho Aria, even when the new trainer, Ricardo Braganza, arrived from Monterrey in his muscular black crew cab pickup with bulging tires. On the next day we met Enrique Camarena when he pulled in through the service gate with his horse trailer and we helped load Martina and her tack trunk aboard. She was not enthusiastic about leaving her friends and family, despite Maya's extensive reassurances.

During that process I saw New Alistair Kingman pass us twice on the other side of the paddock. Walking in a normal gait as if he had never missed a step, he wore his hair freshly parted in the middle in the style of the old Alistair Kingman in the painting. But instead of the knifelike crispness of his ancestor's noble features, Max's fleshy face was a puffy, cratered landscape in which only the blue eyes seemed to have kept their vibrancy. He didn't acknowledge me and I made no attempt to talk to him, even to say goodbye. I suppose I should've felt grateful that he didn't have me escorted from the property. This was the final visit to Rancho Aria for all of us in the Paul Zacher Agency.

Once through the gate at Rancho Camarena, however, Martina quickly perked up and recognized her old pal, Ana, who had formerly boarded at Aria for about five years. They were instantly calling back and forth to each other until we led Martina over to Ana's stall to reconnect. Enrique said he would put them together in the same turn out until Martina settled in.

Maya still rode four mornings a week at the new rancho, set at the edge of the pilgrimage village of Atotonilco. On those days when I occasionally accompanied her out there we always passed the Kingman spread on the Dolores Hidalgo highway. With its magazine cover quality it would have looked just the same to a camera, if not at all to us. I often thought about the drama we had witnessed there. It was a bit of high theater for the two featured players at center stage. And if the characters they portrayed had proven to be flawed at their core, wasn't that what theater had always been about, the often tragic divergence between appearance and reality, about dressing up and strutting about with a few large animals on stage for added impact.

Other, less prominent subplots, like my encounter with Pilar Ruiz, added a touch of comic spice to a drama already rife with its own wry twists and turns.

I could imagine that this long theatrical run before the committed Rancho Aria audience must be why Phaedra had accepted the pretense of Max's immobility for so many years; it was all part of the role he played in this equestrian charade, and when he launched himself from the wheelchair that morning to rescue his crystal trophy, her anger came from the fact that he had for the first time in public stepped out of his part without a script. It was the threat of reality that most offended her, not the ongoing fiction of his life, or of both their lives. I am tempted to read something into that.

In any case, Phaedra stayed on at Rancho Aria. She knew where the money was.

If Delgado had missed most of this, it was not for a lack of seriousness on his part. The fraud of Max's life was a billboard Delgado could not ignore once it was unveiled, and in his cop's logic, it meant Max was suspect number one. He would wear the man down by interrogating him until he cracked. Still, in all fairness, when the truth about Ivan did come out, Delgado did not fight it.

In the weeks that followed I began to appreciate Rancho Camarena as a working spread, where the owners were both active trainers, and where the tone was more serious and more substantial than at Aria. Its atmosphere offered more business than drama, more subtle skills than naughty pleasures. The yard was not a parking place for Mercedes large and small, and the gaggle of six random dogs eager to greet us coming through the gate made an impression more like the Keystone Kops than any fancy Connecticut canine show.

As for the other supporting players, Diana Freeman, the abused ingénue, left Aria soon after we did. While Maya told me she had looked into boarding at Rancho Camarena, Diana ultimately chose to move Pasha to Tolteca, to be closer to the competitions. I'm sure she never knew that her argument with Raul ultimately set in motion the circumstances of his death. I could imagine how mixed her reaction might be.

Drake Wilson, in his role as the devoted, if none too astute, family retainer, stayed on with the Kingmans, although I'm not sure whether he and Pilar ever got together again. Probably nothing more was possible between them, since she had been seared by the whole experience, and her comments about him had borne the stamp of finality, whatever that might have meant in her spinning universe. She had the density of an atomic nucleus, where electrons and protons were spun off constantly at an alarming rate. As I recalled my brief time talking to her (how could I not?), it seemed like she was far more likely to pick up someone new, and it would not take her long to do it. Pilar was a woman doomed to wear her emotional and physical needs on her sleeve, where they could be seen by any man foolish enough to think he was ready for her, or she for him. I wouldn't be surprised to meet her in another case somewhere down the road.

While I didn't expect to see her again any time soon, I couldn't help but imagine painting her, and it will be no surprise that I've thought about Pilar more than once since that day of our conversation. I realized that while Maya was the kind of woman that I tended to affirm and applaud, Pilar invoked in me the desire first to protect her, and soon after, to protect myself, a different prospect entirely. I had glimpsed the first part of that right away at the party, as I recalled, in the softness of her mouth and in her way of speaking. At our later meeting there was often a subtle hint of fear in her eyes, one that surely heralded a layer of terror not far beneath. I now believed the source of that terror came from within her, not the people around her. Was that what made Raul so eager to trap her in his web? I already knew what a fool he was, but this connection would have been, in the end, his undoing if Diana Freeman and his own lack of restraint hadn't finished him first. Once he had Pilar, I could scarcely imagine what followed. None of us had wanted to explore his photo records in search of more data on Pilar Ruiz. Deep within those private images lay chaos, and at this point in the case, all we wanted was peace and the sense that once again we could be confident that we knew what we were looking at.

On a more self-contained note, Renée Bontemps also remained at Rancho Aria. I could not help but see her as a complete contrast to Pilar, although no less passionate in her own, very rationally French, way. No stranger to drama and flawed characters, she would have found the Kingman world more comfortable than we did. She had, after all, dodged the wiles of Raul Sanchez, and beyond his vain attempts to seduce her, she may have found nothing else to worry her there. In her business she was accustomed to drawing firm boundaries around the physical demands of randy men. I never had a chance to ask her why she had betrayed Maya to Licenciado Según. It may have been that in her profession, keeping on the good side of the police was simply prudent business. Whatever the truth was, she had her own sufficient reasons, I'm sure, and there might come a time when I could enjoy exploring them with her.

Two months later we saw her again on a bright Saturday morning during a dressage event at Tolteca. Maya pointed her out to me as she rode up to the judge's stand on Camembert, but across the ring, without letting on, I had already spotted her gold and amber curls trying to flee her helmet.

"Now that you know a *leetle* more about riding terms, I suppose you would say that Renée has a fine seat," Maya said to me with one eyebrow raised.

I nodded slowly. "One of the best I've seen."

The author would be most grateful if you would post a brief review of this book on his Amazon pages.

Please visit the author's website at:
www.sanmiguelallendebooks.com

www.ingramcontent.com/pod-product-compliance
Lightning Source LLC
Chambersburg PA
CBHW030937260626
47169CB00002B/511